MURDER AT MILLAR'S HOTEL

LADY ELLEN INVESTIGATES

KELLY MASON

For Soraya
Thank you for messaging me every day
and keeping me on track
Love you x

CHAPTER 1

The train chugged along the countryside. Having begun our trip at Ashcombe, we had passed Bristol and were now travelling through fields towards our destination of Branden Bay, the seaside town I had chosen to be my home for three months. My ancestral home was undergoing renovations and I was making the journey with my maid, Hetty. We watched the farmland scene from the window with the Mendip Hills in the background. I loved the movement of the train, as it rocked and shunted along, reminding me of the trips I'd taken here as a child with dear Papa, the Earl of Ashcombe. When he died, Papa left me with the responsibility of Ashcombe Hall and the lands that went with it. I could have taken the trip via road, as Branden Bay was only twenty-five miles from Ashcombe Hall, but I longed for the nostalgia I associated with the railway.

I leaned against the seat as foliage brushed the

windows and the sun peeped through the leaves. I shut my eyes and relaxed. Having worked so hard for the previous six years, I needed a rest. I had not wanted to close the convalescent home I had opened in 1918. It had given me a sense of purpose. Every day I kept the home open was a day I did not have to consider my own life and my own future. Even though many years had passed since the conclusion of the conflict, I continued to take in those men still suffering the effects of war, when other convalescent homes had long closed. Many ex-servicemen were suffering from what they called 'shell shock'. The decision had been made, though. My home would become a home again. And leaving Ashcombe Hall while the final renovations were made was the sensible thing to do. It was not only Ashcombe which needed a new lease of life, I did too. I had spent most of my twenties chained to the day-to-day workings and management of the home and now it was time for me to take a step back and assess my life and what I wanted from it.

I returned my gaze to the inside of the compartment. It was a smart cabin with polished wooden walls and plump, newly-refurbished seats. I shook my head as I observed my maid. Her skin was pallid and she had a pained expression upon her face. The poor young woman had already made three visits to the on-board lavatory.

Taking a deep breath, I tapped her knee. "You are quite ill and must remain on the train and return to Ashcombe Hall."

"I can't leave you, my lady," Hetty said and then hiccupped.

"I'm a grown woman approaching thirty and quite capable of looking after myself." I tilted my head to the side. "Mrs Dawkins put pressure on both you and I, when she insisted you accompany me on this trip." My housekeeper had always been a force to be reckoned with. "You have your wedding arrangements to attend to. You're to be married within a month and, as you know, I intend to be away for some weeks. You will have to return before my stay comes to an end."

"But it's my job, my lady," Hetty protested.

"If I need a maid, I'm sure the hotel will provide one," I said, although secretly I relished the idea of simply being alone without anyone fussing over me.

Hetty lowered her head before placing her hand to her mouth. I knew she would rather be at home and had an inkling that it was not motion sickness which ailed her. The sooner Hetty was married, the better.

I leaned forward and lifted Hetty's chin with my gloved hand. "We both know that I would rather be alone."

"But you need me," Hetty said.

I leaned back and smoothed down my black skirt. "Return to the hall, look after yourself and prepare for the wedding. Maybe bring it forward?" I raised my eyebrows.

Hetty blushed.

At this point, my dog, Prince, who had been sleeping at my feet, lifted his head and looked up at my maid with a low woof. He was a red-haired Irish Setter, never leaving my side since the day I rescued him from a fate many runts met as a puppy.

I passed an envelope to Hetty. "Here's a letter for Mrs Dawkins." I had written it whilst Hetty had visited the lavatory. "You will not be in any trouble, and I will pay you throughout my absence…" I trailed off, not wanting to acknowledge the obvious.

Hetty smiled and took the letter. "I understand, my lady. The past few years have been so busy – sharing your house with so many people."

"Precisely." I knew Hetty would not protest for long. She was clearly struggling with what appeared to be an extreme case of morning sickness. I picked up my dog's leash. "Prince will look after me, won't you, boy?"

He barked on cue.

Hetty smiled. "Thank you, my lady."

The train reached Branden Bay Station with a squeak of its wheels and a hoot of its horn as steam passed the windows.

The guard opened the carriage cubicle. "Do you need help with your luggage, Lady Ellen?"

"Yes please," I replied with a smile then gestured towards Hetty. "My maid has been taken ill, so will be returning to Ashcombe Station." I turned to Hetty. "As soon as I reach Millar's hotel, I will place a call through to the hall and get word to George to meet you at the station." The train would be in Branden Bay for half an hour before making its homeward trip back to Bath, via many stops, including the one in Ashcombe village.

After saying farewell to Hetty, I stepped onto the platform with Prince on his leash, feeling thoroughly excited for my solo adventure. As much as Ashcombe Hall was a part of my life, I had longed for this break.

I took a deep breath as Prince tugged on his leash, following the porter who had now overtaken us as he wheeled my extensive luggage on a large trolley. One of the bags contained a bone that my cook had provided for Prince. He sniffed at each of the bags in turn. I guessed he was eager to sink his teeth into his treat.

As I reached the motorcar, which the hotel had sent to collect me, I glanced at the luggage, realising it would take more than one trip to transport everything. Prince would certainly not fit inside.

"I'll take a walk to the hotel," I said to the driver who stood by the passenger door. "I need to exercise my dog."

I tipped the station porter and began the long stroll to the hotel, following the street signs to the promenade. I would be taking the long way so I could pass by the beach. I had visited the picturesque seaside town recently when choosing a place to stay for my extended trip, so I knew my way around. As I neared the seafront, I filled my lungs with seaweed-tinged air and then slowly exhaled the life I had left behind. Alone, except for Prince, I felt freer than I had done in years. I wanted time for myself, to spend money on my own experiences, to blow away the remnants of widow-hood. Other than the dress I wore, I had left my black clothes at home, never before finding the right moment to put them away and bring colour back into my life. But I was sure that grieving for six years was long enough. Indeed, many I knew who had been widowed during the war were already remarried. My darling Leonard would not have wanted me to wither away.

As I reached the seafront I paused, taking time to gaze at the busy promenade and then further out to sea. I smiled as I watched the waves travelling up yellow sands. *I have arrived*, I thought. Prince sniffed the base of a notice board to my right, upon which was a poster advertising the local music hall, situated within the confines of the fairground. As the wind blew, I heard an array of noises and clashes of different tunes drifting over from the fairground. I turned to the sound of screams and I watched the rickety roller coaster rise and fall. I planned to live a little whilst in this vibrant town and especially planned to visit the musical hall to enjoy the enter-tainment. I had not visited a music venue since Leonard had passed and fully intended to book an evening at the venue. I studied the poster which showed the headline act was an entertainer called Mae Grey. I had heard reports of the singer who had burst onto the scene post-war and had seen her picture in the newspapers a few times. She was a thoroughly modern woman with bobbed hair of the fairest blonde. My own hair was a darker blonde, pinned back and long.

Prince tugged at the leash and I remembered that I should make haste and reach the hotel to place a call to George so that he would pick Hetty up from the station. I walked past the pier as visitors to the town swarmed off, having arrived by way of a steamship which was hooting its horn, after filling up with new passengers. With it being the start of summer, the town was bustling with people and everyone seemed to be in high spirits. I felt the collective joy permeate my body and I smiled as Prince pulled me onwards, nearly wrenching my arm from its socket to get to the golden sands. I laughed as I sped up, looking forward to wearing less fussy clothes than the black dress I currently wore. It wasn't floor-length, but it certainly was a lot longer that those worn by the other ladies around me, whose dresses had much shorter hems. I had decided to follow fashion and had commissioned a whole new collection for myself, which I hoped had already reached the hotel.

As the wind blew, my hair escaped the pins which Hetty had placed in it for me. *I'm in need of a new look,* I thought. *If 'The Bright Young Things' can have fun and push the boundaries, then why not me?* After all, I had earned a period of fun, unlike some of the spoiled youngsters I had heard stories about.

"You'll have to wait, Prince," I called to my dog as I restrained him. "We cannot turn up to the hotel covered in seaweed and sand." It had taken some persuasion for the hotel to allow me to bring Prince for my stay. I passed the other hotel I had considered staying at. It was called The Grand Hotel and had four levels with huge bay windows, sitting proudly opposite the promenade. It was where I had stayed with Papa on our visits before the war. It was traditional, in contrast to the hotel I had chosen. Millar's was a fashionable and modern property, furnished to such a high standard that visitors came from far and wide to stay there. It had been hailed as the reason Branden Bay had been revived as a fashionable resort. Indeed, I was lucky to have been able to reserve a room for an extended period.

As I tugged Prince in the direction of the hotel, I passed a barber shop. They had always been the domain of men, but now women flocked to barbers for the new bobbed style. I stopped and looked in the window at the pictures of women with various hairstyles. My hair, now completely loose, flew in front of my eyes.

"You after a cut?" The barber smiled at me from the doorway.

I glanced at my watch. "Do you have a telephone?"

"That I do, miss."

"I would be interested in your services, if you would allow me to make an important call. Is my dog permitted inside?"

"Yes to both. Come on in," he said.

I smiled as I followed him over the threshold and felt as if this was the first step to the new Ellen.

CHAPTER 2

J had called Millar's to collect me and I
travelled in their motorcar with Prince
beside me for the last stretch of my journey to the
hotel. The barber had convinced me that with my new
hairdo I should arrive in style. As the driver reached
the hotel, I gazed up at the impressive white-washed
façade with its huge windows. We stopped underneath
the canopy which covered the grand entrance. I exited
the car with Prince who appeared just as excited as I
was about our adventure. Before entering, I caught my
reflection in the windowpane. The barber had created
a neat bob and had shown me how to style it, as well as
selling me a selection of products to help with this.
With the haircut and unexpected styling lesson it had
taken a little longer than I had expected, but at least I
had been able to speak to Dawkins by telephone to
arrange for Hetty to be picked up from the station.
Dawkins was far from pleased that I had asked Hetty to

return to the hall and suggested she join me herself. I had shuddered at the thought and I feared that I may have offended her with my rather hasty response that I did not require her services. But at least she would not be travelling to Branden Bay.

I entered the lobby with its black and white tiled floor, polished wood reception desk and gold fittings. It was extremely modern, in a fashionable style and was in the perfect location, set high up overlooking the bay.

"I hope your paws are clean," I whispered to my dog as I patted his head.

A stout man, in a suit approached and I recognised him as the manager I had met during my previous visit, when arranging my stay. "Your ladyship, I'm so pleased to receive you."

"Thank you, Mr Breckon. I'm pleased to be here."

Mr Breckon glanced over my shoulder. "Where are your staff?"

"My maid sadly had to return to Ashcombe Hall, due to poor health. I'm here only with Prince." I patted my dog's head, noting with relief that he was on his best behaviour.

Mr Breckon looked down his nose. "Ah yes, he's very welcome. We can provide you with whatever assistance you require and the kitchen staff have been advised to provide his meals."

"Is it possible for me to meet the chef?" I asked, being rather particular about the food Prince consumed – especially as we would be sharing a room.

He did sometimes have a rather unfortunate digestive issue if he ate the wrong foods.

"It's our cook, Mrs Lloyd, who has been given the task, rather than the chef."

"I would like to check exactly what she's planning to feed him, as Prince does have a tendency to react poorly to certain foods." I did not elaborate.

"Indeed, of course you can. Is there anything else I can arrange for you?"

"No, but I'll let you know if the need arises."

"Come this way." He approached the hotel reception desk where a young woman dressed in the hotel's stylish green uniform sat. "This is Lady Ellen of Ashcombe Hall."

"Pleased to meet you, my lady. Welcome to Millar's Hotel," the young woman said in a stilted fashion. Her eyes were slightly red as if she'd been crying. "My name is Olive Cox and I hope you enjoy your stay with us. If there's anything you need then let me know. We have been excited to meet you."

I laughed. "I think I may be a disappointment."

Prince barked.

"And likely a nuisance guest," I continued, "seeing as I have my noisy pet with me."

Olive held up a key on a shiny silver ring. "Your suite is on the third floor and your luggage has been taken up."

"Thank you." I smiled at the sorrowful looking member of staff, her pleasant words juxtaposed by her sad eyes.

"I have arranged a pot of tea, your ladyship," Mr Breckon said from behind me.

I spun around and regarded him. What I really wanted was to change into a dress where the hem came just below the knee and my arms were free to feel the sea breeze. Ideally, I would take tea in my room and relax with Prince. I was surprised that the manager of a hotel so modern could be this awkward. I then realised that maybe it was my presence that was making everyone nervous. I decided that if I was to remain there for three months, I had better put the staff at ease. Thus, I decided to entertain his wish to drink tea. It would be the ideal opportunity to calm the man down.

He led me through the entrance hall to a beautiful orangery which overlooked manicured gardens with bushes in bloom and small palms.

Breckon motioned for me to be seated.

I sat down and removed my gloves. "This is a very special welcome, Mr Breckon, but I was rather hoping to blend in."

Prince sat by my side staring at a plate of biscuits and licked his lips with his huge, pink tongue.

"We pride ourselves at Millar's on a first-class service." Breckon leaned forward to pour my tea.

I laughed. "I'm here to escape the pomp. Please, do take tea with me," I said after noticing with surprise that there was only one cup.

Breckon's face turned a deep shade of red.

I felt guilty, having clearly embarrassed the poor

man, and leaned back in my seat. "I'm here for maybe as long as three months, while the final renovations of Ashcombe Hall are completed. And please, while I'm here, call me Lady Ellen, rather than *your ladyship*. I do not wish to be overly formal."

"As you wish, Lady Ellen."

"Have a biscuit and tell me all about this stunning hotel and the town."

Breckon sat back. "The town was built by the Victorians who came here for health reasons to bathe in the waters and breathe the clean air. Once the railways reached Branden Bay, it brought everyday folk, like my relatives, from Bristol. Since the war, modern buildings have been added, such as this hotel." He appeared to relax once he was in his stride. "It was built upon the grounds of a children's home which was demolished."

I glanced around the glass room, in which there were tables and a variety of plants. "It's an amazing building, I cannot wait to explore. I gather the town is rather lively."

"Indeed, Lady Ellen. It's popular with the youngsters and many jazz bars have opened in recent months. If any of the young set trouble you or you need a quieter room, do let me know."

"Not at all, Mr Breckon," I said. "I intend to live a little whilst I'm here. Fun and relaxation is just what the doctor ordered." It was true the family doctor had suggested I distanced myself from the stresses and upheaval of the renovations.

"I understand, Lady Ellen, that you helped with the war effort?"

"Indeed, I did, and Ashcombe Hall is now being turned from a convalescent home back into the grand building it was before the war. And then I must decide its future. This extended stay in Branden Bay will enable me time to breathe a little and to look at life – objectively. I would like the hall to be of use rather than merely a home for me. Although I do employ many staff and have active farmland."

"We will make your stay as trouble free as possible, and you have one of our finest suites." I had chosen the room myself when visiting for the day to plan my trip. A suite was more fitting and, of course, I had Prince to accommodate.

Prince lifted his head and barked as if reading my mind.

"You will have to do less of that, boy," I said to my dog. "Otherwise, we'll be evicted." I patted his head, feeling his sleek fur brush against my hand.

"What breed is he, Lady Ellen?"

"He's an Irish Setter, but with unconventional looks," I said, looking into the non-symmetrical face of my beloved companion. "They called him the runt but he's the most handsome dog in my eyes." I smiled at Breckon. "My husband also did not have conventional looks." I laughed. It was good to be able to think of Leonard with affection. The knot which had formed in my stomach the day he died had burned until I'd cried every night for three years. Over six years had passed and it had since dissipated, leaving me with fond memories to hold in my heart forever.

"I was sorry to hear of his passing," Mr Breckon said.

"Time is a healer," I said. "I miss him every day. The war was cruel for taking so many of our men. That's why I did as much as I could to help those injured heal."

"And I'm sure they are most thankful to you. My cousin found himself at Ashcombe Hall and spoke of his time there with much fondness."

"There is no need for thanks from anyone. I was able to help, due to the circumstances I was born into. It's the young men who fought, and their families, that need the thanks. I'm immensely fortunate." I sighed. It was something I told myself every day, even though I had often felt a slave to Ashcombe Hall and at times had longed for anonymity.

I stood up and Prince rose too. "I have taken more than enough of your time, Mr Breckon. I would like to be shown to my suite."

"As you wish, Lady Ellen." He gestured towards the reception.

Back at the desk, I watched the line of customers checking in. Olive attended to them and I could not help but notice that she was red-faced and appeared flustered.

As Mr Breckon led me towards the sweeping stair-case leading upwards from the ground floor, I realised it was unlikely I would be treated as just another guest.

"I would recommend the lift, my lady," Breckon said

gesturing towards the elevator. "It's sturdy and engineered to top standards."

"I would very much like to take the stairs. I'm not sure Prince will be fond of such an enclosed space."

I took the sweeping marble staircase, which had a large window on each half landing.

I stopped as I heard Breckon panting behind me and turned. "Take the lift, Mr Breckon. I'll meet you at the top."

He hesitated as if to protest, then bowed and walked back down the stairs towards the lift.

As I ascended, excitement filled my chest. The sense of freedom was overwhelming. As much as I loved Hetty, I wanted to be alone, to be one of the crowd and, hopefully in time, to get lost in it, to be the carefree woman I used to be, before I inherited Ashcombe Hall.

When I reached the third floor, I felt a little breathless. Breckon was already standing to attention at the top.

"Please feel at ease, Mr Breckon," I said, wondering whether he had been in the forces himself at some point, because he stood just like a soldier would. Although he was surely too mature to have fought in the most recent war.

"It's this way, my lady." He walked through an open door and I followed him into the large airy space, which I planned to be my home for the coming months. My luggage had been delivered to the suite and was neatly stacked. The walls were decorated in green upon which was a shimmering gold asymmetrical design. The afternoon sun streamed in which brought a smile to my face. I knew I had made the right decision as I unclipped Prince's leash. He settled on a rug in front of the fireplace, as he always did back at Ashcombe Hall. I wandered over to the window. Outside was a large balcony with a table and four chairs.

"The views from here make this suite one of our most popular," Breckon said from behind me.

"It's stunning." I opened the glass doors and stepped outside and took in the view of the horseshoe-shaped bay, with the pier jutting out to sea. At the end of the pier was a steamboat leaving, no doubt full of travellers. "Where do the boats go?" I asked.

"To nearby Bristol and over to Wales, my lady. It's very popular with day visitors."

"I think I would like to take such a trip myself."

"We can arrange that for you. Let Olive know."

Most of the buildings I could see were Victorian, made from the grey and red coloured stone which I knew had been brought from the local quarry.

"Are you planning to dine with us this evening?" Mr Breckon asked me.

"I was considering room service," I said.

"You may wish to join our other guests as we have entertainment. One of our guests, Mae Grey, has agreed to sing for us on her evening off. She's currently touring the country and is over at Branden Bay Music Hall this week."

"She's staying here at the hotel? How lovely," I said.

"I hear she has a beautiful voice. At what time is she singing this evening?"

"Mae will perform from half seven and we break for dinner at eight o'clock in the Seaview Restaurant. Would you like me to reserve a table for you?"

I considered it for a moment. "Yes, please do make a reservation."

Prince barked.

"I'm sorry, boy. But you'll be remaining in here." I laughed. "I would like to speak with your cook soon, about Prince's food?"

"I will send Mrs Lloyd up immediately. She once had a dog of her own and will be honoured to prepare his food and will bring it up to you. She is an amazing cook." Breckon appeared to be extremely proud of his staff and that was nice to witness.

"Please ensure that a service charge for the cook is included."

He gave a nod. "I will send someone up to help you unpack."

I shook my head. "There is no need for that. I would very much like to do that myself."

"As you wish."

"Thank you, Mr Breckon for making me most welcome."

Breckon left the room and I returned to the balcony and gazed outside. Prince rose from the rug and followed me, sniffing through the sleek railings as my eyes wandered the horizon, then back along the waves to the shore and to the road leading up to the hotel. I noticed a man with a walking stick and smiled as I experienced a burning sensation in my solar plexus. Whenever I saw a man with a stick, I always remembered Captain Ernest Hamilton.

Hamilton had been one of my first patients and it had caused a bit of a stir back at the hall when I had taken it upon myself to nurse him back from the brink. It appeared that a friendship between a captain and a young widow of the upper classes was viewed as entirely inappropriate. I had to admit, I had been rather naïve at the time. Although nothing at all untoward had occurred between us, I had held him in high regard. I sighed, remembering how angry I was when he had been sent away. I'd often wondered about Hamilton. *He's probably married with a family by now,* I thought as I rubbed Prince's fur.

I had resigned myself to being a widow for eternity because I had not met any gentlemen of my own class that I cared to spend time with. Leonard and I had been soul mates and I guessed that the price one had to pay for such a beautiful love was the extreme pain that comes when we lose the one that captured our heart.

I returned inside and looked at the huge pile of luggage.

Prince sniffed at the bag containing the bone I had brought from Ashcombe and whimpered.

"Now, to unpack," I said as I patted Prince's head. "And I may let you have a chew on that bone."

CHAPTER 3

I stood against the railings on the balcony of my suite, looking out to sea. I had enjoyed the process of unpacking which reminded me of myself as a child, filling up the little wooden playhouse Papa had built me within our private walled gardens. He had given me the perfect childhood – as perfect a childhood as I could have had after losing Mama. I wondered whether the fact that Papa had never remarried had affected my choice to shun all male attention since I had been widowed.

The breeze picked up and my powder blue dress fluttered. It was lightweight with a drop waist skirt and I felt thoroughly modern in it. It certainly felt good to be out of the black. I had worn mourning clothes for too long. I moved away from the railing and sat upon one of the four iron chairs which surrounded a circular table. Prince trotted over to me and sat by my feet, chewing on the bone which I had given him to keep him quiet as I unpacked. Mrs Lloyd, the cook, had been up to the room and I was expecting a huge meal for Prince for the early evening. Hopefully, that would send him to sleep and leave me able to enjoy the hotel entertainment and my own fine meal.

There was a knock at the door and I rose from my seat and walked through the suite. I opened it to find a man dressed in the hotel's green uniform with a trolley containing a bounty of pastries, cakes and a large pot of tea.

"Afternoon tea, with the compliments of Mr Breckon, my lady," the man said.

I laughed. "I'll be outgrowing my clothes by the time I leave Branden Bay if you keep spoiling me like this. Please tell Mr Breckon that there's no need for such excesses." I doubted these extras would be charged to my room and I had no wish to be given the royal treatment. But I still stepped to one side to let the waiter push the jangling trolley through the doorway. The cakes looked a little too delicious to refuse.

Prince left his bone on the balcony and entered the room. He woofed and chased his tail in excitement, knocking a flower arrangement from the table in the process. I reached for the vase of flowers, saving the ornate glass from smashing, but the contents continued their journey, landing on the modern and visibly new rug.

"I'm so sorry," I said as I held the vase in my hands, staring at the stems and petals scattered in a puddle of water.

"No problem at all, my lady," he said. "I'll send someone up to clean."

After he left, I wagged a finger at Prince. "You must learn to behave whilst we are here. I have no wish to abuse the hospitality of the hotel."

Prince whimpered, clearly aware that he was being given a thorough ticking off.

I replaced the vase on the table. "Come here, you oaf," I said as I crouched down and gave him a hug, then leaned back as he attempted to lick my face. Standing up, I decided to clear the worst of the mess myself, until I heard another knock at the door.

As I opened it, a maid appeared before me. She was a young woman with tied back hair underneath her white cotton hat. Her face was flushed in sharp contrast to her white uniform. She had an eager look in her eyes.

"I'm here to clean, my lady?" she said in a surprising accent for the area. I would have placed her in London rather than Somerset.

"Come in. I'm Lady Ellen, and your name is?"

The girl's eyes widened. "Lottie Penny. Pleased to meet you." She smiled as she spoke in a slow fashion, as if practising her elocution. Her blue eyes were clear and bright. "I understand there was an accident?"

I gestured to the rug. "I've collected the flowers and put them in the bin and mopped the rug with a towel. Unfortunately, my dog is still learning his manners."

Prince bounded over to Lottie.

"He's a handsome dog," she said with a huge smile.

"Thank you so much. Many call him ugly," I said, feeling instantly warmed by the girl's enthusiasm.

"Ugly? He's beautiful." Lottie gave Prince's back a stroke.

He jumped up at her and she giggled and took a step backwards. A few strands of her light brown hair escaped her small white hat.

"He clearly likes you," I said with a laugh, feeling heartened not only at Prince's joyful behaviour but that he had put a huge smile on Lottie's face, too. "Please take tea with me, Lottie."

"Tea? My lady, it isn't proper," Lottie said in a loud whisper, her eyes wide open, but clearly relishing the idea of joining me.

"Nonsense. I'll shut the door."

"I'll get into trouble," Lottie said although her face displayed pure excitement.

"I often take tea with my staff back at Ashcombe Hall. Without them, I would be quite detached and lonely." My mind wandered back to Ashcombe. I certainly had acquaintances of my own class on nearby estates but none I chose to spend time with, other than out of duty. "I'm a widow."

"I'm sorry, my lady, for your loss." Lottie lowered her head.

"It was six years ago. And I'm out of the black clothes." I looked down at my powder blue dress. It made me feel so different. "Do you have love in your life here in Branden Bay, Lottie?" I motioned for her to take a seat.

She plonked herself down. "No. But I'm to be married."

"To someone you have no feelings for?" I seated myself on the settee beside her. I wanted to know more, always finding the lives of others fascinating. I had to confess, it was part of the reason I enjoyed spending time each day with my staff at Ashcombe Hall, to find out what was happening in the village. Although some people described me as nosey.

Lottie's eyes filled with tears.

I felt callous for prying and decided not to press the girl further. "You can tell me about it on another occasion." I did not want to upset her. She had such a joyful air about her, which was surely not something I wished to snuff out. I gestured around the room. "I think, at present, we both need to enjoy this suite, the view, and the glorious sunshine."

"Yes, my lady," Lottie stammered.

"Let's eat this exquisite spread outside." I stood up and grabbed the handle of the trolley and pushed it towards the balcony. Lottie helped me set the tea and cakes on the iron circular table and then sat down as Prince sniffed her shoes.

"This is so lovely," Lottie said as she stood at the railings. She turned around to face me with a huge grin upon her face. "If it was my room, you'd never be able to move me from here." She sat on an iron chair then took the cake, which I handed to her on a china plate. "Thank you...my lady."

"Tell me, Lottie, do you like working here?" I asked.

"It's a lovely hotel, my lady, but I miss my home."
She took a bite of the Victoria sponge.

"Are you from London?" I asked.

She nodded as she finished the cake in her mouth.
"Yes, I was in service in Mayfair. She took a sip of tea.
"During the war we – and the family, of course – spent
time in the country. That was nice, too. The family
were kind to me. I've been ever so lucky, really. I had a
better childhood than most. I've been in Mayfair for a
few years now, and I loved it there." She sighed. "I
dream of going back."

"So why come here?" I asked.

There was a distant knock at the door.

Lottie looked fearful. "They're probably after me."

"Finish your cake whilst I check who it is," I said.

I opened the door and found a woman standing in
front of me. She had grey streaks in her dark brown
hair and was slim. She was probably in her mid-forties
and she wore a crisp green hotel uniform with her
hands clasped in front of her waist.

I smiled at her. "Can I help?"

"Mrs Flint, my lady. I wanted to check on you
because I sent our cleaner up some time ago?" She
pointed to the cleaning trolley in the corridor. "I hope
she's not being bothersome."

"Not at all. Miss Penny has been incredibly
thorough."

Lottie appeared behind me with the flower-filled
waste bin in her arms and the sodden towel I had used
to mop up the water. She looked down at stray crumbs

on her uniform, then gave a small smile, her eyes shining beneath long lashes.

Mrs Flint raised her eyebrows. "Only timely work is fitting for Millar's Hotel," she said to Lottie.

"As I said, I'm very impressed with her work." I smiled at Lottie and gave a nod of encouragement.

"Thank you, my lady," Lottie said as she left the room and placed the bin and sodden towel on the trolley, then pushed it away, following the stern Mrs Flint along the corridor.

I sighed as I shut the door. I felt ill at ease with the part I played in the class system, where people felt obliged to treat me as if I were the better human being. I had rather liked Lottie and the energy she had exuded. I decided to invite her for tea again – I was intrigued to hear her story. I could tell that behind Lottie's eyes there was much to be revealed and I did so like to hear true stories of real people and their lives. I knew I had a gift for encouraging others to open up and had often wondered whether work on a newspaper would have suited me. But, since Papa had passed away, my world had taken another direction as custodian of Ashcombe Hall.

I returned to the table on the balcony, doubting that I would be able to finish the array of cakes and sandwiches the hotel had provided. However, I was determined to try. A bell rang and I realised it was the telephone. The only other place I had seen a telephone in a hotel bedroom was at the Savoy. I stood up, and approached the table upon which it was perched.

I answered it. "Yes?"

"Lady Ellen," Olive said in a stilted voice. "We have a gentleman who wishes to meet you in the reception." She sounded a lot less friendly than she had when I checked in.

I frowned. "And who might that be?"

"Major Albert Coltrane." Her voice wavered down the phone.

I shut my eyes and groaned. *What on earth is he doing here?* I thought. *Is it not possible for one to get away from Ashcombe and be anonymous?* And of all the people! I felt anger rising from my gut and realised I would have to compose myself to enable me to deal with the insufferable man. "I'll be right down," I said in a clipped tone, intending to put Coltrane in his place. He was a man I despised. A man who felt the need to constantly pursue me, even though I had told him, in no uncertain terms, that I would never be his wife. We had once been engaged, before he had disgraced himself with another woman – a dancing girl in London. Since my dear Leonard's untimely death, Coltrane had pursued me for a reconciliation. But Major Albert Coltrane was the last man I would want to be with.

Prince rose from the carpet and growled, sensing my anger.

"You can't come, boy. You need to stay here and behave." Prince had already bitten Coltrane once before and Albert had threatened to shoot my dog if he so much as nipped him. I patted Prince to calm him, checked my reflection in the mirror and then left the room.

As I stepped inside the lift, I did my best to quell the anger rising within me.

On the ground floor, the doors opened and Coltrane swung around to face me.

"Ellen, you look more beautiful than ever," he said. "Quite the fashionable lady about town. And so nice to see you out of the sombre clothes and at last ready to move on with your life." He ended his list of compliments with a suggestive smile.

I baulked as Coltrane appeared to imply that I was ready to accept his advances. "What are you doing here?" I enquired of him in a less jovial tone.

"Let's take drinks in the orangery." He gestured towards the glass conservatory. "I'll order Champagne."

"Please answer my question." My voice echoed around the reception and I took a deep breath as I noticed Olive widen her eyes from the desk, her face was flushed. This was not the behaviour I wanted to resort to but Coltrane always stirred anger in my heart.

"Dawkins told me that your maid had returned to the hall. By a serendipitous coincidence, which neither of us should ignore, I was also travelling here today."

I counted to three slowly as I felt my heartbeat quicken. "I've told you repeatedly, Major Coltrane – we are not friends. I do not wish to associate with you during my stay here, or at any time." I hoped he was only staying for a few days.

Olive stared at us from the desk as if she was about

to burst into tears, clearly not knowing what to do. I needed to have this conversation with Coltrane in private really. However, at the same time, I had no wish to be alone with the fellow.

It was not only Olive who observed our conversation as others in the reception area began to stare at us. I turned back to Coltrane, keen to close the exchange. "I would appreciate it if you left me alone and returned home."

"As I said, my stay had already been arranged. You can check my booking with the girl at reception." Coltrane raised his eyebrows. "Now tell me you did not know that I'd be here."

"I can assure you, Major, that had I known you were a regular visitor to this hotel, I would have stayed at The Grand."

Coltrane gave a deep, throaty laugh. He put his hand up to his mouth and coughed, dealing me a waft of stale cigarette smoke. "You have to ask yourself, why is there always tension between us?" He gave another suggestive smile which I found nauseating.

I clenched my teeth, inhaled and took one step backwards. "You were responsible for the death of my husband." I heard a few sharp intakes of breath from onlookers who were clearly listening in.

"It was a stray bullet. It could have come from anywhere." Coltrane shook his head. "It's preposterous that you continue to defame me."

"So why exactly were you court-martialled?"

Coltrane lowered his voice. "We've been through

this many times, my dear. They were looking for someone to blame. And the Colonel hated my father."

I was not taken in by his excuses. It was likely that the Colonel in fact liked his father as Coltrane had been let off without charge, even though the evidence pointed to him. "Just leave," I said and about-turned.

"I'll be here for a week. I'll blend into the background and will respect your wish for privacy. But if you need me, I'm in room eleven," he said, following me. He lowered his voice as he reached my side. "It's so nice to see you, Ellen. I hope that, one day, I will regain your trust and we can be as we used to be – years ago."

I turned and shook my head. "Never. Keep away from me." I realised my voice had again echoed around the reception. I turned and took the stairs, chastising myself for having lost my temper with the man.

As I reached my room, tears of anger smarted my eyes and Prince rose from the rug. I sat on the settee and he rested his head upon my lap looking up at me with his faithful eyes. I rubbed his fur, feeling the anger subside as I did so.

After five minutes had passed, I rose and went to the balcony with Prince at my heel. I leaned against the railing as Lottie had done and watched the seagulls flying high.

I lifted my arms out as if I was soaring. "I wish I could be as free as a bird," I called to Prince. For all my money and privilege, freedom was something I had never been afforded. "I think we must travel, and see the world," I said to my dog. "We should have gone further afield than simply the nearest coastal resort." I had picked the town as it would be easy for me to travel back to Ashcombe should a catastrophe occur. I re-entered the suite and approached the wardrobe, wishing to find something stunning to wear for the show that evening. I wished to indulge in a cocktail or two.

That will cheer my mood, I thought to myself. I took a deep breath and relaxed as I breathed out slowly. I could handle Coltrane. I had done so for years.

CHAPTER 4

*J*sat before the modern dresser in my suite. Three mirrors looking like three tall buildings provided reflections at different angles. Luckily, my hair was still in place. The barber had done an exceptional job. I smoothed it with a comb and then added a little Brilliantine wax to tidy a couple of flyaway hairs which had appeared, probably from the moments I had stood upon the balcony admiring the view of the bay. I smiled at my reflection, feeling a surge of independence.

I rose and glanced at the dress I had chosen to wear. It was green, not dissimilar to the walls of my room, edged in gleaming stitching with gold fringe from the drop waist to the daring knee-length skirt. As I stepped into my dress, I was reminded of myself as a teenager, a debutant hoping for a suitor. Now all I hoped for the evening was to be entertained and to be anonymous for a while. *Oh, no,* I thought, realising that as independent as I wanted to be, I required help with the fastening of the dress. It had certainly been designed for a lady with a maid. I walked to the telephone table with the back of the dress gaping open.

I waited for an answer.

"Olive Cox, how may I help you?"

"This is Lady Ellen. Is it possible to send Miss Lottie Penny to my room? I have travelled without my lady's maid and am in need of assistance."

"Lottie? She's a chamber maid," Olive said in a surprised tone.

"I'm fully aware of that fact, but I feel most comfortable with the girl."

"As you wish, my lady," came Olive's clipped reply.

I guessed that Olive no longer approved of me since my outburst in the reception, as all pleasantness had escaped her voice.

I waited until there was a knock at the door and opened it to find Lottie beaming at me.

"Come in," I said. "I hope I have not put you in an awkward position."

"Mrs Flint says I think I'm above my station."

"For helping me into a dress?"

Lottie followed and shut the door behind her.

"I have history. I… Well…" she trailed off as I faced her.

I wanted to know more. "Tell me all about it," I said and then turned to show Lottie my back. "Can you fasten this? I probably could manage it at a stretch but don't wish to pull a muscle or ruin the dress."

"It's very beautiful, my lady. You look like a star."

"Thank you. I had it made by a new fashion house in Bristol. Now, do tell me all about your history," I said.

Lottie fastened the dress, hooking it from the bottom to the top as she told me her story. "I fell in love with the son of the family I worked for, in Mayfair. And he loved me, too. His family found out and I was brought all the way here, to the other side of the country. My aunt's friends with Mrs Flint and I'm to be married to her son, Joseph Flint." She stepped back. "There you are, all done."

I spun around. "And what is Mrs Flint's son like?"

"Joe's nice enough, but I don't love him at all. And he doesn't love me neither." She sighed. "But he's not a strong man. He does whatever his mother tells him."

"It's your life, Lottie. No one can force you to marry this weak man. So, tell me, for whom did you work in Mayfair?" There were a few families I knew there.

"The Marquis and Marchioness of Bandberry."

"Really?" I said and was genuinely surprised. I felt a little sad for Lottie. There was not a small gap between their social class, there was a gulf.

Lottie nodded.

"I know them rather well," I said. "I take it you fell in love with Sebastian?" He was also known as The Earl of Garthorn and was heir to his father's title of Marquis.

Lottie gave a shy nod. "The family were happy for me to play with him as he was an only child. But not when we became older. They sent him to boarding school and forbade him to ever see me again after they caught us...embracing. But we always met up when he came home."

"And the fact that he's banned from seeing you makes him want to see you more?" I said.

She lowered her eyes. "Everyone says I'm a fool to think that he would love me."

I realised I may have come across as being somewhat cynical.

She glanced up, catching my gaze. "But he's been writing to me. He says he doesn't want me to marry Joe."

I raised my eyebrows and doubted very much there would be any future for Lottie and Sebastian. However, that was no reason for the girl's family to marry her off to the son of a family friend. "I agree, you should not wed Mrs Flint's son."

"I have caused my family so much shame, marrying Joe is the only way they'll accept me back. And if I don't, I'll lose this job and have nothing."

I glanced at the clock. It was already a quarter to eight. "We shall speak of this tomorrow. But now, I will enjoy the entertainment the hotel has to offer."

"Mae Grey is on tonight," Lottie said. "She's staying with us, I've not seen her yet, as she keeps to her room, but I heard she's got an amazing voice."

"Indeed, I'm rather looking forward to it." I glanced at Prince. He stared up at me with his big, brown, uneven eyes. "There's something you might be able to do for me, seeing as you like this room so much."

"Of course, my lady, what do you need?"

"Could you be a dear and sit with Prince for me?"

"I'd love to, but I might get into trouble," she said.

"I'll call down to reception and let them know that I asked you to stay."

"Thank you, my lady, for being so kind."

"You need to be kind to yourself, Lottie." I smiled at her.

As I left the room, I decided that I would be taking young Lottie under my wing.

I APPROACHED THE DINING ROOM, at least twenty minutes late for the entertainment, and heard the beautiful voice of Mae Grey floating towards me. Her reputation was indeed warranted and the tone of her voice gave me goosebumps. When I reached the doorway, I stood outside the room, not wishing to disturb the love song Mae was singing.

The room was set out with dining tables covered with white cloths and silver cutlery. At the far end, huge floor to ceiling windows captured the view of the sun as it lowered in the sky. Mae was standing in the middle of the view and was even more of a beauty in the flesh, with thick hair of the fairest blonde I had ever seen, cut into a graduated bob. She wore a black dress with gold fringe and a matching fashionable headband. She stopped after the chorus and smiled at the pianist.

Gosh, I thought as my gaze rested on the gentleman playing piano. I recognised him as Gilbert Barry, a well-known stage actor. I had seen him myself in London's West End. I did not realise he was also gifted at the piano keys. He was an attractive middle aged man with a moustache.

I turned as a delicious aroma teased my senses. A hostess trolley with a large tureen of soup had been wheeled next to me.

"Ah, Mrs Lloyd," I whispered, recognising the cook who had visited my room earlier with Prince's food. Instead of her white kitchen uniform she was dressed in waitress attire. "Thank you ever so much for Prince's food," I said in a quiet voice, so as not to disturb the performance. "He wolfed it down."

"Such a lovely dog, my lady," she whispered back to me with a flushed face. "My Rex loved that mix. I miss him so much." She looked at her trolley. "I'd better fetch the bread." She bustled away.

I turned back to the room and spotted Mrs Flint just inside the door. Her hands were up to her cheeks, watching the entertainment as if mesmerised. I had to agree: the singing was simply beautiful.

I glanced back at the large tureen holding the soup and could not resist lifting the lid. *It looks like pea and ham,* I thought as a waft of deliciousness teased my senses. *My favourite.*

"Can I help you, my lady?" Mr Breckon had

appeared at my side and spoke in a low voice.

I replaced the lid and smiled at him. "The soup smells divine. I already miss my daily bowl. The cook back at Ashcombe Hall makes soup for me every lunchtime.

"I hope you will find Millar's a home from home, Lady Ellen," he said with a smile. "Mrs Lloyd is an amazing cook." His face flushed.

Mae finished her song, ending on a daring high note and we both turned to watch.

Breckon noticed the housekeeping manager inside the door and frowned. "Mrs Flint," he hissed at her.

She turned, looking flustered, and rushed to leave the room. She was a lot less bolshy than the woman I had encountered early.

"I suggest you buy a ticket for the music hall," Mr Breckon said as she passed. "We are fully booked. You need to be at the reception desk."

Mrs Flint left without comment.

The audience clapped.

"This way, my lady," Breckon said as he led me into the dining room and to a table to the far right of the window. The seat not only afforded me an unspoilt view of the bay, with the orange sunset, but also complete visibility of the whole dining room. I surveyed the room as a waiter came over and poured me a glass of champagne. The smile soon slid from my face as Major Coltrane stood up. He was seated at a table close to the entertainers and he applauded Mae Grey with his eyes fixed upon her. I opened my gold embroidered fan from my bag and peered over the top, fearful that if Coltrane turned around, he would notice me.

Mae Grey's expression told me she was less than impressed by Coltrane's excited applause. He was clearly enamoured by her, but through my life I had learned that Coltrane was drawn to any attractive woman. Mae closed her eyes and appeared to take a deep breath before opening them again, her actions telling me that she found Coltrane tiresome.

Mae gestured towards her pianist and spoke in a low, husky voice. "Thank you, Gilbert, I'm flattered to have you accompany me."

"A man of many talents," Coltrane shouted out with a slurred voice.

I groaned. Coltrane had clearly drunk too much – so much so that he was swaying.

Olive from reception entered the room. Her face was again flushed and I wondered whether the girl was right for this job. She was continually flustered. She passed through the restaurant until she reached Coltrane's table and outstretched her hand to him with a piece of paper. He ignored her. Olive gave her head a small yet noticeable shake then placed the note before him on the table.

As she left the room, Mr Breckon addressed the diners from the front. "Thank you to our special guests, Mae Grey and Gilbert Barry. The meal will now be served and Miss Grey and Mr Barry will resume their performance at nine o'clock."

As everyone clapped, Breckon gestured for Mae and Gilbert to follow him to a table, which was the opposite side of the window to mine, but as there was a slight curve to the façade of the building, I could see them clearly. As they passed Coltrane, Mae completely ignored him and he resumed his frantic clapping. Gilbert stopped to speak to him, I assumed to ask Coltrane to restrain himself. Coltrane spoke back to him then threw his head back and laughed.

I leaned back in my chair and pulled my fan up to my face and peered over it, in case Coltrane should look around. As inquisitive as I was, his business was of no interest to me.

Gilbert seated himself next to Mae on the table set for two. Breckon stood with one hand behind his back and the other holding a bottle as he poured champagne into wide rimmed glasses. I picked up my own glass and took a sip of the fizzy liquid, feeling the bubbles tingle in my mouth as I stared at the back of Coltrane's head. He remained standing and I couldn't help but notice how his hair had been swept to the side in an attempt to cover his balding scalp. I amused myself with that fact, knowing how vain my one-time fiancé was. Attractive looks really had been all that the major had to offer, and they were fading.

Coltrane gestured at Mr Breckon as if he was a mere servant. Flinching, Breckon approached Coltrane. Frowning, Coltrane thumbed his own chest, as if demanding something. Mr Breckon's face deepened to a dark red and he looked to the next table, maybe not wanting others to hear Coltrane's words. He nodded at Coltrane and stood tall, as if on parade, then about-turned and brusquely walked away, his face like thunder.

There was one thing for sure, I wasn't the only person in England who despised Major Albert Coltrane. I truly hoped his stay at the hotel would be brief.

Coltrane lowered himself to his table and plonked himself down. I was of the impression he'd had too many pre-dinner drinks. He picked up the note which Olive had left on his table, shook his head then crushed it in his hand before dropping it to the floor.

I looked towards Mae and Gilbert. They were smiling at each other with much affection. I frowned. I was sure Gilbert was married and he was also much older than Mae. *Interesting,* I thought as my inquisitive streak took over. I turned back to glance at Coltrane who was staring at Mae with a scowl upon his face. I narrowed my eyes, attempting to figure out his expression. As I did so, he moved his head a few degrees and caught my eye. His lips grew into a slow smile as soon as he recognised me. He rose from his table. I groaned and glared at him. He paused. I shook my head, but he continued to approach me.

I fluttered my fan as he reached my side. "Major Coltrane, it seems you have been drinking."

"A little too much whisky. Good stuff. The hotel manager might be useless but he can choose a good malt." He leered at me with a lopsided smile. "Ellen, you look more beautiful than ever. Would you mind if I joined you?"

"I would indeed mind," I said in a hushed tone. "I thought I had made it quite clear to you this afternoon. I've already said everything I could ever possibly say to you, Major Coltrane. We are not friends and I have no wish to interact with you in any way whatsoever." I did not think I could make it plainer to the man.

"Please stop this nonsense. It's clear we two are meant to be together. We have been brought here by a fate you must not deny."

I sighed as I looked past the major to see Norma Lloyd, the cook, ladling the starter into his bowl. "Your soup will be cold if you do not return to your table."

"Will you join me?" he asked, swaying and reaching out to the chair beside him to steady himself. "It's ideally placed to watch the show."

"Please leave me alone." I rose my voice then took a deep breath. Yet again, eyes were upon us.

"Do as she says, Major."

I felt a shot of pins and needles up my arms, recognising the voice instantly. I turned my head. Before me was none other than Captain Ernest Hamilton, leaning on his stick. A stick that I had gifted him myself and had once belonged to Papa.

"Ah, ha," Major Coltrane slurred, looking from me to Hamilton then back to me again. He steadied himself on the chair as he began to sway even more, using his other hand to point at me before belching loudly.

I closed my eyes. *Was I really once engaged to this hideous man?* I thought.

"This is why you want me to leave you alone!" Coltrane's voice boomed across the room.

I looked around as a hush fell and fluttered myself with my fan, wishing I could hide behind it.

"You're here for a liaison with Captain Hamilton," Coltrane slurred. "It's all becoming clear. You scandalous woman."

I opened my eyes, now feeling unable to speak.

Coltrane gestured at Hamilton. "This man is not of your class."

I shut my eyes, not bothering to point out to Coltrane that he also was further down the pecking order. But he had never accepted that, having a dubious link to a lord somewhere in Yorkshire. It was so far removed that it was a miniscule claim, but it somehow gave him an elevated position in society. The restaurant hubbub petered out until it was silent apart from the clang of cutlery.

I spoke in a measured tone. "This is the first time I have set eyes upon Captain Hamilton for more than five years. I had no idea he would be here."

"This is absolutely true, Major," Hamilton said. "Now, please leave Lady Ellen in peace, we have an audience." He gestured around the room. "Show some respect."

"You'll regret this, Hamilton, you blighter." Coltrane turned and staggered away.

I motioned for Hamilton to sit opposite me and

looked around the room as extra waiting staff entered to help Mrs Lloyd with the soup. "I can't believe you're here," I whispered.

"It's so good to see you, Lady Ellen."

"Are you here with your wife?"

"No, I have not been blessed with a family life. I'm taking a break between jobs." He gestured to his table. "I've been sitting over there, alone, transfixed, wondering whether it was indeed you. Your hair is different."

I touched my new bobbed style. "I had it cut today by the barber here in Branden Bay. I'm still getting used to it and have been feeling somewhat self-conscious."

"It suits you, my lady." He looked over to Coltrane. "When I saw the major harassing you I had to step in. I hope I have not embarrassed you."

"Not at all," I said. "Although his reaction was unwarranted, I would have left the room embarrassed by the major, had you not been here."

"I take it your engagement did not work out?" he asked.

I took a deep breath. "Major Coltrane and I were betrothed before I married Leonard. I understand he told you back in Ashcombe that following Leo's death, he was going to rescue me and we were to be wed. I'm afraid to inform you that Major Coltrane lied to you and we were not courting."

"I'm sorry," Hamilton said. "I should have checked his story before leaving. But I felt it was for the best for me to go. For your reputation, my lady. With you being vulnerable, having only just lost your dear husband and being the lady of the hall."

"Time has moved on, Captain Hamilton." I picked up my glass of champagne. "Do ask the staff to move your place setting to this table."

"Are you sure?"

"Of course." I motioned to a flustered looking Mr Breckon who was passing. "Captain Hamilton will be joining me for dinner."

He called a nearby waiter who then set a place for Hamilton at my table as we watched in silence.

I glanced over to Coltrane as he lifted his spoon. "I hope he chokes," I said and noticed the surprise on the face of the woman sitting at the next table. Yet again I had spoken a little too loudly.

"I could not agree more," Hamilton said. "What a despicable man he is."

Coltrane began to cough loudly.

"Oh dear," I said, as a small laugh escaped. "I may have had my prayers answered." But my laughter soon faltered as Coltrane's face turned a deep purple and he began to splutter.

Breckon rushed over to him as our fellow diners stopped eating and watched on.

Coltrane clutched his throat and gasped as if his windpipe was blocked. He turned and stared directly at me and outstretched his arm, as if wanting to reach out to me and pull me close. His eyes bulged, then his head fell face down into his soup.

CHAPTER 5

*B*reckon placed a hand on Coltrane's neck and felt for a pulse. He gasped. "He's dead." The whole scene looked like an amateur theatre production and I felt as if I was detached, watching from a distance, not quite connecting to the reality of the situation.

Breckon stepped back and made the sign of the cross. Coltrane's body slid from his chair then fell with an unceremonious thud to the floor as a few nearby diners screamed.

I stared at Coltrane's lifeless body, speechless and unable to process what had happened. The man I hated, who I had blamed for my husband's death, was spread on the floor, covered in pea and ham soup. Coltrane was not quite forty and seemed too young to be dying of a heart attack, yet he had always been one for excesses. Excessive drinking, excessive food and, as

I had found out when betrothed to him, an excessive hunger for women.

Hamilton stood up. "Excuse me, my lady." He walked across the room with his stick as I watched on.

Breckon stood still, with his face bright red and eyes bulging open, nearly as wide as Coltrane's had before he died. "I'll call the police," he said. "Will everyone please leave the room and give the poor man some respect."

"My good man," Hamilton called out to Breckon, reaching him then turning to address the room. "I'm afraid the police will want everyone to remain exactly where they are." Hamilton placed a hand on Breckon's shoulder as if in an effort to calm the poor man down.

With the room silent, I heard the footsteps of someone approaching and Olive entered the room. The receptionist put her hands to her face, stared at Coltrane's lifeless body and let out a piercing scream.

I put my hand up to my ears and the hubbub returned to the room as everyone turned and stared at the poor girl, tears pouring from her eyes.

Breckon marched towards her then ushered her out of the room. "We need to call the police," he said to her. I shook my head. Even when the poor girl was distressed he was ordering her around. A few others rose from their seats.

"Everyone, stay where you are," Hamilton said, in a voice befitting of a captain comfortable with ordering his troops, as he guarded the body.

I spotted Gilbert attending to Mae who appeared to

have swooned. She came to with her hand to her brow. Gilbert escorted her towards the exit with the help of one of the waiters while everyone remained silent. Hamilton did not insist they stay, since she clearly needed assistance.

"It's awful," Mae said with a hand to her chest as she passed through the room.

Gilbert had his arm around her. "At least he won't bother you again."

Norma Lloyd stood nearby to my table, next to the hostess trolley. "God moves in mysterious ways," she muttered to herself but loud enough that a few diners overheard and gave her a disapproving look.

I watched as Hamilton stooped and picked up a crumpled piece of paper and put it into his pocket. I realised it was the note Olive had brought in for Coltrane. I caught his eye and gave a small nod. Hamilton was clearly as inquisitive as I was.

Others, having left their tables, were standing at the edges of the room, discussing the incident in hushed tones. One young woman cried as a gentleman consoled her. Guests began to chat amongst themselves and Hamilton returned to my table.

We spent some time speaking to those nearby, saying how unfortunate it was, until three uniformed officers entered.

One gestured towards Coltrane. "Ryan, check the body."

"Yes, Sergeant Chambers," he said as he crouched before Coltrane's remains.

What a way to die, I thought. Coltrane was clearly drunk before the attack and I wondered whether his demise was due to ill health or whether he had indeed choked on his food.

A woman on the next table to us stood up. "It was him," she shouted, pointing directly at Hamilton. "I heard them arguing and he threatened him. He killed him."

Hamilton shook his head. "I was here on the other side of the room and I didn't touch the man."

The woman then pointed at me. "She said he was going to choke to death." She looked back at the sergeant with her hands to her chest. "They poisoned him."

I shut my eyes, feeling everyone stare at us. I had no wish to join in with this charade. I rose from my chair and covered the width of the room until I reached the sergeant. "I can vouch for Captain Hamilton, he was seated at my table, beside the window."

"Were you an acquaintance of the deceased?" He opened his notebook.

"He was a neighbour of mine," I said, now wishing that I'd remained at my table as I did not wish to be interrogated.

"So, Miss... What's his full name?"

"Look here, Sergeant," Hamilton said having joined me. "Lady Ellen is not a 'Miss'. Please address her appropriately."

Before the sergeant could speak, I replied. "The deceased was Major Albert Coltrane, son of Major

Alexander Coltrane of Ashcombe Manor. Ashcombe is some twenty-five miles from here."

"I know where it is." He turned to Hamilton. "And how did you know the victim, sir?"

"I met him briefly, some years ago," Hamilton said. "I'm not an acquaintance of his."

He gestured at his officers. "Jones, you and Ryan – get everyone's names and addresses." The sergeant turned to us. "You two are coming to the station."

I felt incredibly tired. "Could this perhaps wait until the morning?"

"Lady Ellen has had a shock," Hamilton said. "And Major Coltrane was clearly suffering from ill health. It is unfortunate, but the fellow was drunk, which clearly exaggerated existing ailments."

The sergeant sighed. "I take it you're not a doctor, sir?"

"Well…I…"

"The doctor will arrive soon and if he considers the death suspicious, it won't be me you'll be answering to, it'll be Scotland Yard."

I truly hoped that would not be the case. My trip to Branden Bay was proving to be far from the relaxing break I had yearned for.

"I'll come to the station and give you the facts," Hamilton said. "I'm sure there is no need for both of us to attend."

Fortunately, the sergeant agreed, and Hamilton followed him out of the room. He looked over his shoulder at me and even though I was standing only a step away from Coltrane's body, I felt a warmth cover me and smiled at him as he left.

"Name?" the officer called Jones asked me as he approached.

"Lady Ellen Tamar of Ashcombe Hall." A few people looked my way. *So much for being anonymous,* I thought.

"Thank you. And how long will you be staying at the hotel?"

"I'm a long-term guest," I said, although I was having second thoughts. This was not exactly the best start to my stay.

"Please make your way out of the room, my lady. We may be in touch later for questioning." Jones turned to the next diner to obtain their details.

I left the room and found myself in the reception. I felt numb, wondering whether it was the adrenaline pumping through my veins dampening my emotions or whether I really cared not a jot that Coltrane was dead. One thing I knew for sure, I needed a cup of tea and the company of my dog.

I turned as I heard a woman wailing and looked over to the reception desk to see Olive being comforted by Mrs Flint who patted her back.

"Pull yourself together. I know it's shocking, and I was fond of him too, but we have jobs to do," Mrs Flint said. "The Millars will be back soon and we need to handle this matter with care as custodians of their hotel while they're away."

I guessed it was the first time Olive had seen a dead man. Sadly, I had seen a few myself. – the poor men who had stayed at my convalescent home and not made it. Maybe that had anaesthetised me to the sight of the dead. I had sat with a few of the lamentable men, some still so young, during their last moments, imagining I was with Leonard, saying goodbye. I blinked away a tear, but it was not for Coltrane. Death always reminded me that I was a widow.

A queue formed at the lift, many gossiping about the dead man, so I decided to take the stairs, eager to escape the crowd.

When I arrived at my suite I knocked, as I only had one key and had left that with Lottie so she could take Prince for a comfort break.

Lottie opened the door and greeted me with a smile. Prince barked and jumped up as soon as he saw me.

"You're back earlier than I expected." Lottie frowned. "Is everything all right, my lady?"

"Unfortunately, there has been a commotion downstairs. A guest, a man I knew called Major Albert Coltrane, had some sort of attack and ended up face down in his soup before slumping to the floor."

"You mean he's dead?" she whispered.

"Yes, I'm afraid so."

"I'm so sorry, my lady. What a shock to lose a friend like that."

"He was no friend." I plonked myself down on the settee. "I have already been accused of his murder."

"He was killed?"

"My dear, people love drama." I shook my head. "He

appeared drunk. Major Coltrane was a man of excesses and they caught up with him."

"I'll go down and fetch you a sweet tea, my lady."

As I waited, Prince laid his head on my lap, looking up at me with doleful eyes. He clearly sensed my shock and I stroked him absent-mindedly.

"My lady, your tea?" Lottie had let herself back in and was trying to pass the cup to me. "I brought some brandy too, if you'd like some. Mrs Lloyd suggested it."

As I took the tea, the cup rattled on the saucer.

"Do you want me to stay awhile?" Lottie asked.

"Would you? That's so kind."

She sat beside me. "Did you know the man well?"

"Believe it or not, we were once engaged."

Lottie took a sharp intake of break. "No wonder you're so upset."

I took a thoughtful sip of my drink. "I'm quite sure that I'm not upset. The man killed my husband." I felt myself shiver. "But I'm in shock."

"Here," Lottie said, "let me help you to your bedroom."

I let Lottie, who was more than ten years my junior, take the lead.

Later, as I drifted off to sleep, one question was printed on my mind – *did someone indeed kill Major Coltrane?*

CHAPTER 6

*R*ays from the sun rested on my eyelids but it was not the light which had woken me. Prince barked as raised voices came from the living area of my suite. I pulled on my silk housecoat and padded to the door but refrained from opening it as I listened to an exchange between Lottie and Mrs Flint.

"Do not argue with me, Charlotte. Get to your room and wash. You have cleaning duties to attend to." Mrs Flint's voice was loud and clear.

Prince whimpered at my feet. I had allowed him to sleep in my room the previous evening in my state of shock.

"But I was looking out for Lady Ellen, she said I could stay. I was worried about her. She's had a shock."

"Haven't we all! A man died last night. At least you didn't have to witness it. Poor Olive is in shock too but she's still assisting customers at reception. You need to leave this room, at once." Mrs Flint paused. "It's just like you to think you're above your station and make friends with a lady."

"I…" Lottie attempted to interrupt.

Mrs Flint continued. "I would have thought after what happened with the Earl of Garthorn, you would have learned your lesson. We do not mix with the likes of them. The sooner Joseph makes an honest woman of you the better. And since it's your birthday today, there's no reason to delay the wedding any longer. Seventeen is an ideal age to start wedded life. I was your age when I married Mr Flint."

"It's my life and my choice," Lottie said.

I bit my lip as I heard Lottie repeat the words I'd spoken to her. I smiled. I had clearly made an impression on the girl.

I opened the door and stepped into the living area, closing the door behind me to keep Prince contained. "Is there a problem, Mrs Flint?"

"My lady," Mrs Flint said. "Lottie is needed – if you can spare her." Her lips formed a straight line on her face.

"I'm sorry, Lottie has been most kind. But she must be incredibly tired, is it possible to relieve her of her duties this morning?"

Lottie's eyes opened wider.

Mrs Flint took a step back as if I had physically pushed her. "I'm afraid not, my lady. We're short-staffed."

"Yes, it's been a shock for everyone, I understand," I said moving towards her.

"An inspector has turned up this morning from Scotland Yard and I believe there may be a message for you at reception," she said.

"So, it was murder?" I wrapped my arms around myself.

"That's not for the likes of me to say," she said.

No doubt I'll be hauled down to the police station, I thought, wondering what time Hamilton had made it back the night before.

Mrs Flint turned to Lottie. "Get to your duties." She looked back at me. "My lady." She bobbed her head, then left the room.

Lottie followed then looked over her shoulder and gave me a small wave with a grin upon her face.

I smiled back at her then closed the door.

Prince barked from the bedroom.

I let him out. "I like Lottie too, boy," I said as I patted my dog's back. "She has a beautiful heart and it's her birthday. I think we need to arrange a gift, don't you?"

Prince barked again.

AFTER DRESSING, I checked my reflection and sighed. I did not have enough time to style my hair, which was no longer in the neat wave created by the barber. I wanted to read the message left for me at the reception so decided to wear a dress with which I had a matching hat. I planned to spend the afternoon practising my hair.

I reached the hotel reception with Prince on his leash. Once I had picked up my messages I planned to take Prince for his walk as he was tugging at the leash to go out. Breckon rushed over as soon as he spotted me, his face bright red. He was clearly feeling the strain. I, myself, felt remarkably calm and knew that was because Coltrane was dead and would no longer bother me.

"My lady, you have a message." He handed me a piece of paper.

"Calm down, Mr Breckon," I said, worried for his health.

He wiped his forehead with his handkerchief, then lowered his voice. "They say it's murder. This isn't good news for the reputation of the hotel. The owners are expected home within a fortnight, they're returning from a trip to Calcutta."

"The hotel has been most successful in their absence, Mr Breckon," I said. "You should feel proud of your achievements and of your staff. This is not your doing."

He replaced his handkerchief into his breast pocket.

I opened up the slip of paper as Prince whimpered. "I'm sorry, my dog is desperate for his walk." I looked down at the paper.

Lady Ellen,
please come to Branden Bay Police Station
at your earliest convenience.
Inspector Stone.

"So much for a pleasant walk," I said. "I can't leave Prince here, he will have to come with me," I added, to no one in particular. I turned to Breckon. "Thank you."

As I walked through the reception area, I noticed Olive, her face red and her eyes angrily staring towards me. The poor girl was clearly still in shock. If she was a member of my own staff, I would have given her the day off, but it seemed Millar's Hotel was being run under somewhat harsh rules. I was rather interested to meet the Millars when they returned.

When I stepped out of the hotel, with Prince on his leash, I immediately felt the sun on my skin. It felt like a brand-new day and as shocked as I was about Coltrane's demise, there was a sense of relief that the man responsible for my husband's death had received his comeuppance. I was sure that the police were being overly cautious. Coltrane probably poisoned himself with alcohol.

After walking Prince, I picked up a small bone for him from the butcher where I asked for directions to the police station.

As I reached my destination, I walked up the steps to the entrance and approached the sergeant who was standing behind the high wooden reception desk.

"Sergeant Chambers, isn't it?" I asked, recognising him.

"The inspector has been expecting you," he said with a sniff. "The prisoner has named you as his representative."

"The prisoner?" I frowned.

Chambers looked at the papers on his desk. "A Captain Ernest Hamilton."

"Hamilton is still here? You've arrested him?" I asked, believing the reason I had not seen Hamilton at the hotel was because he was sleeping in. The calm feeling slowly ebbed away.

"We don't usually allow dogs, I take it you have this one under control?"

"I have brought a bone to keep him occupied," I said, hoping Prince behaved himself.

"If you could come this way, my lady," Chambers said.

I entered the dark interview room, which was empty other than a table and four chairs. I took a seat and pulled the bone from the paper the butcher had wrapped it in and handed it to Prince, who made himself comfortable underneath the table. I turned to my right and stared at the door, waiting for it to open. I had to admit, as grave as the situation was, I did have a flutter of anticipation in my stomach.

The door opened and Hamilton entered. He looked slightly dishevelled in his shirt, which was open at the neck. I suddenly realised how very dashing he was. He had changed a lot since I had last seen him. Back then his daily attire was the pyjamas which I had provided for guests at my convalescent home. His body had often been hunched. But now he was clearly a much stronger man.

I rose from my chair as I noticed Hamilton was in handcuffs. "What is the meaning of this?" I gestured at

Hamilton and then at the police officer who had followed him in. "Why is Captain Hamilton restrained?"

Prince barked.

No one answered my question as I shushed my dog and stroked his head. "It's all right boy, settle down." I returned to the seat.

The uniformed policeman gestured for Hamilton to be seated next to me.

"My lady," Hamilton said, "thank you for coming."

I smiled at him and then Sergeant Chambers entered. He was followed by a tall man with a dark expression, emphasised by dark eyebrows which sat above inky eyes and beneath almost-black hair.

"And you are?" I asked the man.

"Inspector Stone, of Scotland Yard."

"You arrived quickly," I said. "Did you take an overnight train?"

"I was in the area." Stone scowled at me then motioned for Sergeant Chambers to sit beside him.

Stone flipped over the pages of the small notebook. "The doctor has confirmed that Major Albert Coltrane was poisoned, although the exact poison has yet to be ascertained. We have the following information." Stone took a deep breath before relaying the details in a monotone, London accent. "You were engaged to the victim. You broke off the engagement and met The Honourable Mr Leonard Tamar who died in friendly fire during a training exercise. Major Coltrane broke the news to you and attempted to comfort you by offering to wed and care for you."

"And spend my family's fortune. Really, Inspector!" I said and sat back in my chair. "It was so decent of Major Coltrane to offer to take in such a destitute woman," I added in a sarcastic tone.

Prince growled.

Inspector Stone ignored me and carried on. "You started a relationship with Captain Ernest Hamilton six months later, while he was at your convalescent home."

"Not true," Hamilton said. "Lady Ellen was merely attending to me, as any nurse would."

Stone continued. "Major Coltrane and Captain Hamilton nearly came to blows last night in the hotel restaurant."

"That is an exaggeration, Inspector," I said with a shake of my head. Prince gave a low growl from underneath the table and I leaned down and patted his head to reassure him, realising his teeth were rather close to the inspector's leg. I wished I had left him back at the hotel. Prince was far from a vicious dog, but he was a protective one.

"It was merely a conversation," Hamilton added. "Coltrane was an unlikeable chap, but I did not kill him."

The inspector continued without commenting. "Earlier that day, you, my lady, accused Major Coltrane of murdering your husband and stated that he would choke to death."

"My words have been twisted," I said.

"Do you deny that you accused Major Coltrane of killing your husband?" Stone stared at me.

"He was court-martialled, Inspector," I said with a sigh. "I suggest that rather than relying on gossip, you do your due diligence and contact His Majesty's forces to ascertain the facts." I shook my head. "And please, release Captain Hamilton this instant. He's an innocent man."

The inspector flipped over a page. "At Millar's Hotel, diners overheard an altercation between Captain Hamilton, yourself and the victim."

"Inspector, would you not have harsh words for someone who was court-martialled in connection with the death of your spouse?" I paused. "Is this all you have? It's pure hearsay and gossip from guests who were drunk on copious amounts of complimentary champagne."

"And a threatening note was found on Captain Hamilton's person when he reached the station."

"I have already explained," Hamilton said. "I picked the note from the floor." He rubbed his right wrist beneath the metal cuff, with his left hand.

"Even if Inspector Stone believed that," Sergeant Chambers said. "You tampered with evidence."

"I collected the evidence," Hamilton said with a shake of his head. "I would have discussed it with you if you had given me the chance and not treated me like a villain as soon as I arrived at the station, ordering me to turf out my pockets like a common criminal." He lifted his cuffed hands and rubbed his cheek, which I could see was in need of a shave. I felt a blush rise to my cheeks and turned to face the inspector.

I leaned forward. "About five minutes before Major Coltrane's demise, the hotel receptionist brought a note for him." I smiled at Inspector Stone. "I'm sure you'll be able to confirm this with Olive Cox who works at Millar's Hotel."

"Coltrane read the note," Hamilton said. "Then crushed it in his hand and dropped it to the floor. I retrieved it as I thought it might be relevant if the man had not died of natural causes."

"What did the note say?" I asked.

"Pay up or die," Hamilton said.

I turned to the inspector. "I suggest you follow up that lead with the hotel receptionist and release Captain Hamilton immediately. Unless you want me to call the police commissioner, with whom I'm closely acquainted?"

I noticed one of the inspector's large eyebrows twitch. He snapped his notebook shut. "Sergeant Chambers will take your statement, my lady, and then you will both be free to go. However, neither of you must leave town."

I suppressed a smile. That suited me fine, as I had no intention of going anywhere. I intended to find out exactly what had happened to Major Coltrane.

CHAPTER 7

*A*n hour later, myself, Hamilton and Prince walked down the High Street. It was sloped towards the promenade with the sea visible in the distance, which had white crests on the waves. I breathed in the clean fresh air and let out a long, slow breath.

Prince tugged at the leash, dragging me towards the promenade.

I laughed. "I think we need to reward Prince for his good behaviour at the station. I was on tenterhooks, worried he would nip Stone's leg."

"He's an amazing dog, my lady. When did you acquire him?" Hamilton asked. His stick tapped on the floor as he walked beside me.

"I rescued him, the day you left Ashcombe Hall. Prince is nearly six years old. Aren't you boy?" I called out to my dog who continued to tug at the leash. "He thinks he's still a pup though," I said with a laugh.

Prince stopped to sniff a lamppost and I looked to Hamilton and smiled. "I haven't had a chance to say how nice it is to see you again."

"Likewise," he said. "And it is so fortunate that you know the Police Commissioner, otherwise I would still be in there, banged up until that buffoon finds the real killer."

"I must confess, I've never met the commissioner," I said with a laugh. "Indeed, I don't even know the fellow's name. But I doubt Inspector Stone will check."

Hamilton laughed and we continued down the High Street, passing the shops, some of which had queues outside. The town was already bustling.

Do you think Coltrane was poisoned?" I asked Hamilton.

"I've seen a man poisoned before," he said. "It was suicide in his case, and I have to say, the deaths were remarkably similar."

We spent some time in silence, walking single file along the busy High Street until we reached the promenade.

"Are you happy to walk on the beach?" I asked Hamilton since he was still wearing his evening shoes.

"Yes, I've cleaned many pairs of shoes in my time, especially while in the army."

As we stepped onto the sand, the waves crashed towards the shore. It was a blustery day and whilst not cold, the wind had a bite to it, especially when mixed with spray. I let an excited Prince off his leash and pulled my coat collar up to keep the wind from whipping my neck. With my hair much shorter, my neck was exposed more than it ever had been before. I was pleased that I had pinned my hat on tightly.

"I do miss Ashcombe," Hamilton said with a raised voice due to the sound of the surf. "I think of the hall often." He looked at me.

"You do?" I asked, wondering whether it was more than the hall he thought of.

"Daily," he replied.

I felt a bond between us but also had to remember that Hamilton was not of the same class as me. His rise in the ranks of the army was through effort and skill, not because of his schooling and father's connections, as was the case with Coltrane. Although he was a well-spoken gentleman, he was still of a middle-class upbringing. But we were not in Ashcombe, we were in Branden Bay, where class lines appeared blurred within a modern environment away from the traditions of my estate and the village.

I crouched as Prince brought me a stick, smooth from travelling down the Bristol Channel and into the estuary, and threw it for him. With the wind so strong, my voice was whipped away when I tried to speak. We continued the rest of our walk on the sands in silence.

As we left the beach and reached the end of the promenade, Hamilton turned to me. "We will no doubt have to entertain Inspector Stone and his continued questioning."

I nodded. "It will be difficult for us."

"Will you be leaving town? I'm sure the inspector cannot make you stay."

"I, for one, am not prepared to stand by while the whole town gossips and muddies our names," I said. "I think we need to find the killer ourselves, don't you?"

Hamilton hesitated and gazed at me. "I would be most honoured to assist you."

"My opinion is that Inspector Stone is fixated on us and I fear he will be looking at our movements while the real perpetrator escapes."

I looked down as I fixed Prince's leash back onto his collar. "I intend to make my visit to Branden Bay an adventure."

Upon reaching Millar's Hotel, I bade farewell to Hamilton, who went to his own room. Considering he had spent the entire night in the police cell, I suggested he rested and I arranged to meet him for tea in the orangery the following day. I put my head on one side as I watched him walk away with his stick towards the lift. I felt sad that he still felt the need to carry it.

I approached the reception desk.

Olive glanced up, her eyes still red. "Can I help you, my lady?" she asked in a pitiful voice.

"Yes, my dear. Could I order food for Prince?"

My dog barked at the sound of his name.

"Do you think you could arrange for me to meet with Mrs Lloyd?" The first thing I planned to do as part of my secret investigation was to interview the cook, considering she had made the soup which Coltrane had tasted prior to his death.

Olive blinked. "Unfortunately, she's been taken to the police station."

"Oh dear." It seemed that she was the next port of call for Inspector Stone. maybe the man wasn't a complete buffoon considering I had wanted to speak to her myself. I guessed that with Hamilton out of the cells, Stone had decided the cook was his new prime suspect. "Hopefully she will be back soon," I said in a breezy tone, but I doubted it. I was of the opinion that the police felt most comfortable with at least one person in the cells assisting them with their enquiries. "I would like to take luncheon in my suite."

"Of course, my lady," Olive said in a quiet voice, still avoiding eye contact with me.

"Could you please ask Lottie to bring my meal up for me and one for Prince?" Hopefully someone else in the kitchen would also know how to prepare a meal for a dog.

Olive nodded without protest.

I was not particularly hungry but wanted to share lunch with Lottie, I needed to speak to somebody. I was bursting to discuss the case and, with Hamilton resting, there was no one else I trusted.

I took the stairs with Prince but this time when I reached the top floor, even though I had walked at least a mile along the beach, I felt invigorated. Was it the adrenaline from the case? *Or something else?* I wondered, remembering Hamilton. I gave a small smile, realising how pleased I was to find him in my life again.

Once inside my suite, I looked to the balcony, I would not be able to take luncheon there on such a blustery day. Prince settled by the unlit fireplace and I waited for Lottie and our food.

There was a knock on the door and I answered it with a smile to find that Lottie was not there. Instead it was a stony-faced Mrs Flint.

"I'm afraid Lottie is not available, my lady. She's assisting the chef, considering our cook has been called up to the station to help the police with their enquiries." She made no eye contact with me, her lips again in a thin straight line.

Maybe she thinks it was me that poisoned Coltrane? I thought, remembering that I had overheard Mrs Flint telling Olive that she was fond of him.

"And here is luncheon for yourself and your dog."

I stepped to one side as she wheeled in the hostess trolley with our food.

"Thank you," I said. "But surely Lottie can have a break?"

Mrs Flint took a sharp intake of breath. "As I said, she's working. If that will be all?"

"Indeed, it is. Thank you, Mrs Flint."

"My lady." She turned around and left the room.

Inside my suite, I lifted the cloche from Prince's plate and watched him wolf the food down in double quick time. He proceeded to lick the plate so hard it moved across the room. I smiled as I watched him nudging the plate as if he was dribbling a ball. My dog forever lifted my mood and had carried me through life since I had lost Leonard. But I found myself not at all hungry for my own food. I stood up and pushed the trolley into the bedroom, out of the way of Prince who would have enjoyed the cold meat salad. I pulled the door until it clicked shut.

Prince had settled himself on the rug in the main living space and I knew he was ready for a sleep following his long walk and large meal.

"Stay, boy," I said but he was already snoring.

I picked up the room key and went into the corridor, closing the door quietly behind me.

Finding the service lift, I took myself to the ground floor. Once it opened, I did not require directions to the kitchen. Smelling the waft of garlic and hearing the clatter of pots and pans, I found the kitchen door open and walked in.

"Madam, you have lost your way?" the male chef said in a strong French accent.

"Not at all," I said. "I understand you're short staffed and have come to help."

"Not in my kitchen," he replied with a flick of his hand.

Lottie stood up and rushed over to the chef. No doubt telling him who I was – a woman with a title.

He turned and, by his softened expression, it appeared my title had impressed him. "I am most honoured, but I do not think you will want to be in here."

"Nonsense," I said as I approached the sink and washed my hands. "Back at Ashcombe Hall I'm often to be found in the kitchen, helping to prepare the vegetables. I find it therapeutic." I turned around and smiled at the chef. "It's how I discover exactly what's going on." I smiled at Lottie and the woman she was sitting beside. A young man ate an apple as he leaned against a dresser and nodded a hello to me.

I seated myself at the large oak table. "Just humour me, I'm rather missing my staff. I'm lonely." I took a seat next to Lottie. "So, what's your job?" I asked her.

"I have to finish the beans before I'm allowed my break."

I picked up a paring knife. "We'll do this in no time." I began trimming the runner beans.

"Norma likes us to cut them into diamonds," Lottie said. "Like this." She showed me.

"So, when is Mrs Lloyd returning?" I asked.

Lottie shook her head. "No idea, my lady. She prepared the soup you see, so the inspector from Scotland Yard took her away an hour ago for questioning. Mrs Flint heard they're keeping her there..." She mouthed the rest of the sentence, "...in the cells."

"I fear that is my fault. I rescued Captain Hamilton from the cells and assume the inspector has now moved on to Mrs Lloyd."

"Poor thing," the kitchen assistant said as she trimmed a carrot, then sniffed.

"Don't get upset, Polly, she'll be back soon," Lottie said. "Norma's done nothing wrong."

"She won't like it up there," Polly said. "And the food will be awful."

"Did anyone else have the soup?" I asked.

"Yes, plenty," Polly said. "Including me and I've not kicked the bucket."

"I had some," the young man said.

"We all did," Polly said. "Chef, me, Norma and David." She nodded at the young man who had now finished his apple.

"So, if Major Coltrane was poisoned, his soup was likely to have been tampered with after it had left the kitchen." I looked along the table.

Polly sighed. "Norma poured Major Coltrane's soup at his table."

"Oh yes," I said. "So, they think she slipped something into his bowl?"

"She didn't like the man," David said as he launched his apple core at a bin and missed.

"Shush your mouth," Polly said. "Just because she said he was a cheat don't mean she snuffed him out."

"She said more than that about him," the lad said as he picked the apple core up from the floor and disposed of it.

"We don't talk ill of our own, boy," Polly said as she went to the sink. "Just because you crossed her and she roasted you, doesn't mean she's guilty."

David huffed and left the room.

I hoped Norma Lloyd was taking no nonsense from the inspector. I sped up with the vegetable preparation. I wanted to ask Lottie extra questions in private.

"The inspector is likely under pressure to have a suspect behind bars," I said trying to allay their fears.

"He's unlikely to think she poisoned the soup, after all as you said, he was not the only one to eat it." I thought of the delicious pea and ham and cut the runner beans and I felt my appetite return with a vengeance.

"I heard that policeman from London was around these parts on his honeymoon," Polly said with a laugh, seemingly in an attempt to lighten the mood. "I bet his new wife ain't happy."

"That explains how he arrived so early," I said. And also why he was so terribly bad tempered... "We're finished." I stood up and held out my hand for Lottie's.

Lottie looked nervously at the chef.

"Come along, Lottie. Otherwise, Prince will be up to mischief and I need his plate bringing down," I said.

Polly looked back down at her work, clearly not wanting to get involved and have to answer to Mrs Flint should Lottie's absence be discovered.

"Thank you, Chef, for entertaining my wants. I'm most grateful." I smiled at him.

"My pleasure. Are you dining with us this evening?" he asked me.

"I'll be taking my meal in my room." I smiled at Lottie and then pulled her hand as I removed her from the kitchen.

Once in the corridor Lottie put her hands to her cheeks. "Mrs Flint is going to be so cross if I go with you."

"She's a bully and I will not have it," I said as we reached the service lift. "Come along. I will be speaking to Mr Breckon as he is senior to her, it won't be a problem."

I regarded Lottie as the lift made its journey and saw her chewing her lip. "Are you quite well, my dear?"

"After we left your room this morning, Mrs Flint told me she's booked the wedding. She said the sooner I'm wed the better and that Joseph can keep me under control."

"That's absolutely disgraceful," I said.

"I'm not ready," Lottie said as tears ran freely down her cheeks. "For married life."

I was taken aback. "Let's get to the room and talk this through." I was feeling a similar emotion to when I had found Prince at the hands of the gamekeeper.

Lottie blinked away her tears. "My lady, she'll order me away and I'll be married within a couple of weeks. I don't want to annoy her even more."

There was no way I would leave Lottie to that fate. "It's a free country, my dear. Come along." I pulled the lift door open.

CHAPTER 8

*J*nside my suite, Lottie and I were met by a feather-covered floor. Prince thrashed his head from one side to the other as he chewed a long cushion which had originally been placed on the chaise longue. It now resembled a dead serpent.

"Prince!" I scolded. "What have you done?"

Prince stopped and lowered his head, dropping the remnants of the cushion to the floor.

Lottie set about scooping up the feathers as Prince whined and whimpered. Knowing he was in trouble, he took himself to the corner of the room with his tail firmly between his legs.

Once we had tidied the mess, I went to the bedroom, opened the door and pulled the luncheon trolley into the room. "The tea will be tepid and stewed. But let's eat." I was glad that the hotel had, as usual, been extremely generous with their portions. There was more than enough to share.

"I'm not hungry, my lady," Lottie said.

Prince lolloped over from where he had been hiding in the corner of the room and put his head on her lap.

She burst into tears. "Joe's nice enough, but I just can't..." She changed her voice to a whisper. "The wedding night."

I stood up and went to the telephone. I needed to resolve this as soon as possible. Olive soon answered and asked how she could be of help in a lacklustre voice.

"Could I request that Mr Breckon comes to my suite?"

"I'll ask him right away," she said.

"Thank you." I returned the receiver to its rest. "I will sort this, Lottie. You will not be married." I hated to see Lottie's exuberance, innocence and zest for life snuffed out.

"What are you going to say?" she asked with her eyes wide open.

"Trust me, Lottie." I patted her hand. "I will sort it without even mentioning the wedding."

Breckon soon knocked upon the door and I let him in.

"You wish to see me, my lady? Is there a problem?" He still looked flustered.

"Thank you so much, Mr Breckon for taking time to come and see me. I appreciate how busy you are but I have a favour to ask." I led him into the suite and closed the door behind him.

I saw his shoulders droop as he set eyes on Lottie but this did not put me off.

"As you know, my maid was unable to make this trip. Unfortunately, she will be unable to come to Branden Bay at all. So, it is my request that Lottie Penny is assigned to me whilst I stay here."

"Well ... I ..."

"Lottie has a connection with my dog and anyone looking after me needs to have a good rapport with him."

Lottie smiled and rubbed Prince's head and he gave a little whine as he laid his head on her knee.

"Unfortunately, Prince has ruined a cushion." I lifted the bin. "He needs round the clock attention. And I will of course pay for the damage he caused today." I smiled at Breckon. "If you would relieve Lottie of her current employment, without the usual notice period, I will employ her directly as my assistant. It could be for as long as the next three months."

"Please, Mr Breckon," Lottie pleaded.

The manager's face relaxed. He was probably well aware of Lottie's position and I hoped that I had appealed to a hidden soft side.

"Unfortunately, this is a seven day a week job," I added, "and Lottie will be required to stay in the maid's bedroom within this suite." I pointed to the second small bedroom. My aim was to keep her away from Mrs Flint.

Breckon looked harassed and glanced at Lottie and

then back at me as if he did not have the energy to argue. "It's not usual, and I will have to check with…"

"With whom?" I asked. "Surely not Mrs Flint? Lottie is old enough to make her own decisions. Her contract of employment is with the hotel, not Mrs Flint, a member of staff junior to yourself?"

Breckon's eyes darted around the room. His face reddened even more.

"I understand it's hard with Mrs Lloyd in the police cells. Do you think she did it?" I said, baiting him.

"She is the dearest lady you could ever meet," he said with an expression not dissimilar to the one Prince gave me when begging for a treat.

As he had floundered, I decided to ask another question relating to the murder. "While you are here, Mr Breckon, I wonder: what was it you discussed with Major Coltrane, immediately before he died?"

"What do you mean?" he asked with a bluster.

"In the Seaview Restaurant. He called you over, spoke, thumbed at his chest then gestured at you."

"He wanted his room cleaned," Breckon stuttered. "And yes, well done Lottie on gaining the respect of such an esteemed guest." He nodded at me. "I will inform Mrs Flint and the other staff of Lottie's resignation from the hotel and her new position."

"Thank you, Mr Breckon. Thank you so much," Lottie said with her hands held together as if in prayer.

"And Mr Breckon?" I asked.

"Yes, my lady?"

"Do send up the largest cake you have available. After all, I understand it's Lottie's birthday today."

Breckon left the room and I smiled. I had been left with the impression that he had caved to my request for Lottie's services to avoid any further questioning on Coltrane's demise. I needed to find out the full nature of Breckon's dealings with Coltrane, for I did not believe for one moment that Albert Coltrane was simply asking Breckon to arrange the cleaning of his room.

"I'll be such a good worker for you, my lady," Lottie said standing up. "I'll do everything for you."

I swung around. "You are to be my companion and assistant. I'm totally capable of dressing myself, apart from fastening the odd button. And I will dress my own hair." I smiled at Lottie, hoping that was indeed something I could manage. I still had to learn how to style my hair and did not want to wear a hat all day, every day. "Can you read and write?" I asked her.

"Oh yes, Sebastian taught me. He wants to be a professor, so I was his student." She giggled.

"Good, because I want you to help me solve this murder. And I'll be taking you to the music hall this week, as my birthday gift to you."

Lottie opened her eyes wide. "Are you sure?"

"Absolutely. And now, let's finish our food. I'm absolutely famished," I said.

Lottie's appetite had appeared to return as she ate and clearly enjoyed her luncheon. I now had a team.

With Hamilton and Lottie to help me, I was sure we would discover how Major Albert Coltrane died.

As much as I had wanted to be alone when I had originally planned my trip to Branden Bay, I enjoyed a much easier sleep with Lottie in the next room. Not least because Prince had gladly slept in with my new assistant so I had not been kept awake by his snoring or his unpleasant digestive issues.

Before bed the previous evening, Lottie, Prince and I had a pleasant evening stroll along the beach. The wind had dissipated and Prince had bounded up and down, free from his leash. We had returned to the hotel for our meal, which we had eaten on the balcony as the sun set, followed by extremely large slices of cake, which we had devilishly eaten with our hands. Lottie had told me all about her childhood and the time spent with Sebastian. She had certainly seen some of the finer parts of life that would have passed by a regular child growing up in service. I appreciated how Lottie had made young Sebastian's childhood so much fun. She had such energy for life. At the end of her story, I firmly laid the blame for her association with Sebastian with the adult members of both families. Clearly, the Bandberrys were happy for her to entertain their only child. It was akin to where some families had a nanny and then banished them when the children were grown. Upset always followed.

There was a knock on my bedroom door which brought me back to the present.

"Yes?" I called from my bed.

"I've collected your breakfast, my lady," Lottie said from outside my room.

I pulled on my housecoat and opened the door. "That's very kind of you, but it is our breakfast, not mine. And if I were to sleep in one morning, there is no reason to wait for me, do help yourself to food."

"After we have eaten, my lady, would you like me to walk Prince?"

"Thank you, that would be lovely." I needed to spend time on my hair. I ran my hand through it, liking the way it felt, free of the long tresses which I used to plait before bed and which were uncomfortable to sleep on.

"And I brought you the newspaper. Major Coltrane has made the front page." She tapped the headline.

"Fabulous."

"Would you like me to pour the tea?"

Prince barked.

"I don't want you to serve me, we will help ourselves. Do tuck in." I gestured at the array of pastries and fruit.

After breakfast and once Prince had bounded out the suite with Lottie for his morning walk, I sat down on the settee and poured myself another tea and picked up the newspaper. The headline stated:

MURDER AT MILLAR'S HOTEL

As I read the piece it was clear that the newspaper

had already decided it was a premeditated killing. It focused on the major's greatest life achievements, all of which were either exaggerated or outright lies. The journalist had clearly spoken to Coltrane's mother, who had forever sung her son's praises. She had, of course, used fabrication because all her son had ever done was disappoint her. The only relevant part of the piece was that a member of the Millar's Hotel kitchen staff was helping the police with their enquires.

Poor Mrs Lloyd, I thought as I put the newspaper down, assuming that Breckon would be livid after reading it. It looked to the outside world like a member of his staff had murdered a guest. It was not the greatest advertisement for the hotel restaurant.

With a lack of any real details in the article, I realised that no one had a clue what had happened. I took a journal from the sideboard, which I had purchased from the High Street during our walk of the previous day, and a new fountain pen and wrote on the inside cover.

Who killed Albert Coltrane?

I was looking forward to my first official meeting with Hamilton and Lottie.

After an hour, Lottie returned with Prince from a long morning walk. I was already feeling accomplished, having successfully styled my hair using pomade before waving it into position with a comb, the way the barber had shown me. I had added a little make-up and felt very much the independent modern woman.

Prince bounded in and barked, demanding my attention.

"Did you miss me, boy?" I asked as I leaned over to scratch his head.

Lottie removed his leash, her long hair windswept. With colour to her cheeks and her eyes bright, she appeared very much the young woman she was and certainly not old enough to start wedded life.

"I'll change, before we meet Captain Hamilton," Lottie said.

"We have another half an hour, my dear." I smiled as I watched Lottie walk into the second bedroom and wished I'd had a younger sister, or any sister come to that. Lottie was different to the other maids I'd had, or any of my staff. I rather guessed that would have been due to the time she had spent with Master Sebastian. Lottie had an ease about her which told me that she had learned to cross the social lines in a natural way. I saw in her what I always tried to impress on my staff at the hall: that we were all human beings. Yes, be respectful to one's employer, but relax, too. We are all but flesh and blood.

CHAPTER 9

As we left the suite in order to meet Hamilton for elevenses, I felt slightly nervous. Or was it excitement? We took the stairs and when we reached the orangery, Hamilton was already waiting for us with a huge smile upon his face.

He stood up as we approached. "I received your message, my lady, that there would be three of us for elevenses."

Prince barked.

"Yes, Prince," I said with a laugh to my dog. "I should have said four of us."

"Shh," Lottie said to Prince. "Else I'll have to take you back upstairs."

Prince obediently sat down.

"We three will be working on the case of murder at Millar's Hotel," I said in a low voice.

"I know a man has died," Hamilton said. "But I do feel an element of intrigue."

We sat down at the table set for three.

"We are fully justified in our quest," I said. "We must clear our names. We can't have people accusing us in public of killing a man and do nothing." I remembered the scene in the dining room the night Coltrane died. I sensed Hamilton felt a little guilty at the excitement created by our planned investigation. I pulled the journal from my handbag. "Can you take notes for me, Lottie?"

"Yes, my lady," Lottie said in her poshest voice as if adopting a new role.

"In your neatest handwriting, please. There's blotting paper inside."

Lottie took the book with a smile. "Of course, my lady."

We were interrupted by a waiter bringing the refreshments I had ordered earlier in the day. A large pot of tea was accompanied by delicious looking shortbread. The waiter nodded at us and left.

"Let's start while the tea brews," I said. "First, we have Inspector Stone's current suspect – Mrs Norma Lloyd, the hotel cook." I turned to Lottie. "Can you think of any good reason she would poison Coltrane?"

Lottie wrote the cook's name neatly under the heading of *Suspects*. "When I popped down to the kitchen, after walking Prince, Polly told me she wasn't surprised the police had taken Norma because she spoke badly of Coltrane. Polly said Norma was pleased he was dead and told everyone as well."

"What reason did she give?"

"Norma apparently said he was an evil liar."

"Did she know him before he visited the hotel?" Hamilton asked.

"He'd been here a few times before I started working here. So maybe she had trouble with him then. But she definitely knew of him before this visit."

"How do you know that?" I asked.

"Polly said Norma once told her that she could tell a few stories about what Major Coltrane got up to in London that would make her hair curl. And that his family were rude and selfish."

"I could vouch for his bad behaviour myself. I wonder when she met his family?" I said. "Who did Mrs Lloyd work for in London?"

"She worked for Queen Mary, my lady. Used to ask her to cut up the runner beans into diamonds, that's why we do it that way here."

"I doubt she met Major Coltrane at Buckingham Palace," Hamilton said. "I can't imagine King George inviting him for dinner."

"I have to agree," I said. "Why did Mrs Lloyd come to Branden Bay?"

"She lost her husband, my lady, and her family are here," Lottie said. "She was born in these parts. That's all I know."

"As soon as she's released, we'll speak to the woman," Hamilton said. "It's a shame the poor lady is in the cells. Bit cramped I found, when I was up there."

"I assume they've yet to charge her," I said. "Next on

my list is Gilbert Barry. I saw him exchange words with Coltrane in the restaurant."

Lottie spoke as she made notes. "He's famous, I doubt we'll be able to interview him."

"Neither of the men looked happy during their exchange," I said. "I want to know what was said. Something to note is that when Gilbert passed me, he said words to the effect that Mae Grey would no longer need to worry about Coltrane pestering her."

"I suggest we speak to the man as soon as possible," Hamilton said.

"Neither he nor Mae come out of their rooms, or eat in the restaurants," Lottie said. "They have room service and are over at Branden Bay Music Hall most of the day. Mrs Flint deals with delivery of their meals herself." Lottie giggled, "She's got a thing for him."

"For Gilbert Barry?" I asked.

"Yes, she's mad about him. She's seen him on stage, up in London and in Bath. She's not been to Branden Bay Music Hall yet, we're too busy so Breckon hasn't let her have time off."

"I saw her in the Seaview Restaurant, gazing at them in awe. I thought it was at Mae," I said.

"No, it'll have been Gilbert. Polly told me the other day, it's driving poor old Flint mad that she can't get to see their show. Norma said Mrs Flint even collected toenail clippings from his bathroom."

I pulled a face. "No wonder she's been in a bad mood with you," I said to Lottie. "If she is so obsessed with the man."

87

"Not half as mad as she'll be knowing I'm off there this week when she's stuck at the hotel."

"Oh dear, yes she may be busier now that I've employed you."

"Oh?" Hamilton asked.

"Sorry, I omitted to explain. I've employed Lottie as my assistant due to a sensitive issue."

Lottie nodded at me. "It's all right, I don't mind the captain knowing." She turned to him. "I'm engaged to Mrs Flint's son and she's been pressuring me to get married soon and I wish to call the engagement off. It's going to have to be postponed now as I'm needed seven days a week to look after Prince." She grinned.

"I see," Hamilton said giving me a small smile. "Well done Lady Ellen on rescuing young Lottie here."

I smiled at my young companion. "Let's go to the music hall this evening. Maybe we can speak to Gilbert and Mae Grey there? I'll pretend to be a huge fan."

Lottie's face flushed. "I can't wait."

"Please add Mae's name to the journal."

"They're definitely both performing tonight." Lottie looked at Hamilton and then to me. "I saw it on the poster when I took Prince for his walk."

"Do you suspect her as well?" Hamilton asked me. "Surely she's no killer!"

"On the night he died, Mae ignored Coltrane in a way that suggested she found him distasteful," I said. "And he clearly had been bothering her from what Gilbert said."

"I wonder in what way Coltrane was bothering

Mae," Hamilton said. "Although, I noticed the man could not keep his eyes off her. Even though she was with Gilbert Barry."

"With him?" Lottie asked with her eyes wide open. "Isn't Gilbert Barry a bit old to be romancing Mae Grey?"

"He's a married man," Hamilton added with a frown, "old enough to be her father. But that does not stop some chaps pursuing much younger women."

"Especially the monied kind of man," I added. "If we attend their show tonight, we can attempt to set up an audience with them both."

"Maybe you two should go and I'll stay here and mind this one." Lottie patted Prince's head as he sat beside her.

My face heated up at the thought of an evening alone at the music hall with Hamilton. "Not at all, Lottie. I already promised to take you as your birthday gift. I think if we feed Prince and give him a large enough bone to chew, we'll be able to leave him here." I stroked my dog. "Hopefully he'll not eat another cushion.

"I believe the three of us will bring different perspectives to this case," Hamilton said. "Three sets of eyes will be beneficial to our investigation. Anyone else you think we should consider?" Hamilton asked me.

"Mr Breckon was not a fan of Major Coltrane. They had a heated exchange at his table. And when I questioned him about it yesterday, he was extremely evasive and clearly chose to lie, saying Coltrane was asking for his room to be cleaned."

"Shall I have a word with the chap?" Hamilton asked.

"If the opportunity arises," I said. "But we will need to approach him softly. I do not wish to upset him and be asked to leave the hotel." I looked out of the orangery in the direction of the reception. "I also noticed that Olive reacted rather badly to Coltrane's death."

"Norma told me Olive screamed," Lottie said.

"Yes, she did," I confirmed.

"It was as if her own relative had died," Hamilton said in agreement, "rather than a hotel guest."

"It was rather dramatic and begs the question: was it put on, to cover up her guilt?" I asked.

"I'll ask around," Lottie said, "to see if she knew him outside of the hotel." She wrote further notes.

"Olive is young," Hamilton said. "She may simply have been upset about seeing a dead body."

"Is there anyone else, my lady?" Lottie asked.

"I think that's enough for now. Let's enjoy our elevenses," I said. "And this afternoon we will have to find something for you to wear that is fitting for a trip to the music hall. We are a similar size. I'm sure I have something suitable." I had brought more than enough clothes and intended to pass a couple of outfits to Lottie, seeing as she was now my companion. I also hoped to find a seamstress to create more clothes for her. I wanted to take a boat along the channel to Bristol and that would be the ideal opportunity.

Lottie blushed. "Thank you so much, my lady," she said in her poshest voice.

I smiled. I enjoyed Lottie's company and was touched by her visible gratitude. I poured the tea after dismissing protests from Lottie.

Hamilton sat back in his chair. "I must say, I'm rather looking forward to this adventure. And as Inspector Stone insisted that I must remain in Branden Bay, I do not feel guilty about extending my holiday in this delightful town."

"What has been your business, Captain?" I asked.

"Security. I've recently been overseeing a house within a forest by Exmoor while the owner has been on an extended trip to Europe. I decided to spend a weekend in this bustling town before going to my next job. However, that has been cancelled due to my restricted travel."

"I'm so sorry, Captain Hamilton. I feel responsible," I said.

"Nonsense, my lady. I've more than enough security jobs lined up around the moors. There has been a spate of robberies over there."

I smiled at Hamilton. He had hardly aged since staying at Ashcombe Hall. Indeed, he looked younger without the frown he used to carry on a daily basis. I wanted to ask whether he had recovered from his shell shock. Hamilton had been so damaged by what he had witnessed during wartime. But seeing that he still carried his stick, which was merely a mental crutch, I knew it was still with him. I was reminded of his night-terrors that had brought us together. *Poor Ernest,* I thought, watching him sip his tea and remembering the time when he was simply Ernest, and I was simply Ellen.

Prince heaved himself up as we ate our delicious crumbly biscuits with our sweet tea.

"You can have a small piece." I broke a biscuit and placed it on the floor for him to wolf up. "Are you missing the beach already?" I turned to Lottie. "If he has two long walks today and double his meal portion this evening, I'm sure we'll be fine for our evening trip to the music hall."

"I'm so excited," Lottie said.

So am I, I thought.

CHAPTER 10

"*I*'m most honoured to be escorting you both this evening," Hamilton said as we stepped out of the lift into the reception area.

I smiled and glanced at Lottie, who I had to admit looked radiant and quite the sophisticated young woman. I had helped to curl and pin her hair so that it looked to be in the style of a bob. It was a special experience for me to do someone else's hair for a change. Lottie was convinced I had discovered a new talent which had made me laugh.

I looked back at Hamilton who was wearing a dinner jacket and white bow tie. His dark hair was neatly styled and slicked.

"And you look exceptionally dapper, Captain," I said with a smile.

We made our way towards the exit.

"It's a touch blustery out there," I said.

"I've arranged for the hotel car to chauffeur us," Hamilton said. "It's waiting for us out front."

We walked through the reception and I noted that Olive was missing from the desk. "Will you wait for me at the door?" I asked Hamilton and Lottie.

I approached the desk where Breckon was shuffling some papers.

"Mr Breckon, is Olive well?" I enquired.

He frowned. "She's feeling under the weather, my lady. But will hopefully be back with us tomorrow." At least it seemed they had given the poor girl some space.

"And yourself? It was quite a shock losing Major Coltrane and it's going to affect everyone."

"I'm more concerned about the hotel's reputation." He shook his head. "Bad news travels fast. I've yet to hear from the Millars, but am expecting an angry call when they dock."

"The papers do so love to have something salacious to report," I said. "I'm sure everyone realises your cook was not the culprit. After all, Major Coltrane was the only person poisoned. I'm sure she will be released without charge."

"Your car is waiting, my lady," Breckon said, clearly unwilling to discuss the topic further and wishing to be rid of me.

I returned to Hamilton and Lottie and the doorman opened the door for us.

"I've not been for a ride in a posh motorcar before," Lottie said in a breathy voice. "Sebastian and I used to play inside his father's Silver Ghost, until we got told off by the chauffeur."

"Who's Sebastian?" Hamilton asked, once we were settled in the car.

Lottie lowered her gaze and bit her lip.

"He holds Lottie's heart," I said, answering for her. "But their relationship is deemed inappropriate because he's the son of the employer she worked for. Hence why she was banished to Branden Bay."

"There are worse places," Hamilton said in a cheery voice.

"I do sometimes feel I perpetuate the divide," I said. "Being of a certain class myself."

Hamilton smiled. "Lady Ellen, you are a blessing and not at all stuffy."

"You're the nicest person I've ever met," Lottie gushed at me.

I laughed. "Now I feel as if I were inviting your compliments. Let's have a most enjoyable evening, where the upper, middle and so-called lower classes converge in joviality." I laughed as the car drew away.

As the chauffeur drove us towards the promenade, Lottie stared out of the window. Spending time with her reminded me to enjoy and appreciate the little things in life and not to take anything for granted. I was aware of Hamilton's gaze but did not return it for fear of catching his eye.

When the car reached Beach Road, which ran parallel to the promenade, I watched the stream of people enjoying the evening. Motorcars and carriages travelled in all manner of directions giving the town an air of excitement. Along the promenade, many were taking evening strolls or heading towards the fairground. I had not seen so many people since my last trip to London. It appeared that after the war years, everyone was living life to the full and Branden Bay was as vibrant as I had hoped it would be.

The car finally came to a halt at the entrance of the fairground and Hamilton jumped out to help me, with his stick underneath his arm. Lottie scrambled out after me and I smiled at her excitement.

"I know we're here to investigate, but let's have fun in the process," I said.

As we entered the fairground, we were met with a colourful array of flags and banners advertising the various attractions, including the show we were attending which was headlined by Mae Grey. The sound of clashing music and laughter made my body tingle and I soaked up the atmosphere. As we made our way through the jostling crowd, I felt a real part of it, rather than on the periphery. Living in the world instead of observing it from afar. I breathed in the sweet aromas coming from the various food vendors selling hot treats. Lottie grabbed my arm as she gazed, wide-eyed at a snake charmer. I gave a hearty laugh. No one had grabbed me like that since I had been away at school having adventures with the other girls.

'I'd love to go on the wheel,' Lottie said once we reached the ride.

'Yes, let's,' I said, looking up at the Ferris wheel, the daylight fading behind it.

"I'll fetch your tickets," Hamilton said, making his way to the kiosk.

As we waited in line with our tickets in hand, Lottie was nearly hopping with excitement and waved at Hamilton who was standing beside a coconut shy. He had declined the invitation to join us on the wheel, considering each carriage only took two people. We climbed inside the gently rocking carriage and the man running the ride closed the wooden door behind us. The ride soon jolted into motion and we were taken up. The town looked beautiful in the darkening evening, with the sun at its lowest, bright lights in the buildings and gas lamps lit in the streets.

"It looks so pretty," Lottie said. "Thank you so much for bringing me here."

"It's your birthday treat, and you deserve it," I said, feeling a similar excitement.

When we reached the top, Lottie waved to Hamilton and he waved back. I smiled down at him.

"I think Captain Hamilton likes you, my lady," Lottie said.

I felt my face redden. "Of course he does. I was his nurse. He is most grateful."

"If you say so," Lottie said.

"Oh, look at the castle," I said, changing the subject. I pointed to the ancient building perched high above the town. "I'd love to visit."

As we descended, I watched a couple of boats

bobbing upon the water before we whizzed past the ground and were taken up again for a view of the town. After three revolutions, we stopped and took our turn to exit.

"Thank you, Hamilton, you must take a ride next time we visit," I said.

"I loved it," Lottie added.

"My pleasure," he said with a smile.

"Let's make our way to the music hall," I said as my heart beat a little faster.

As we reached the entertainment venue, Hamilton stepped forward, insisting that he pay for our tickets. It appeared that everyone wanted to spend their money on me, yet I was the last person that needed charity. It was so odd that as, someone of great wealth, the hotel fed me huge portions of food and provided me with complimentary drinks, which I could well afford, when morally it would be better to give free food and drink to the poor.

"Look at the programme," Lottie said, pointing at a poster. "There are loads of musical performances, acrobats, a comedy show and singers including Mae Grey. It says it's all part of Gilbert Barry's Variety Tour."

"We're lucky to catch her, she may not be here for long," I said, wondering whether Inspector Stone would ask Mae Grey to remain in town. The sooner I found out if she was connected to Coltrane's demise, the better.

Hamilton returned to us with the tickets. "I'll speak to a staff member and try to get you backstage."

Hamilton approached a member of staff. "Excuse me, is it possible for my good lady and her younger sister to see Mae Grey and Gilbert Barry in person, backstage? We've travelled some way to see her." He turned and winked at us then turned back to the man. I noticed Hamilton press a coin into the palm of his hand. Hamilton looked back and beckoned for us to approach as the member of staff left.

"He's going to enquire," Hamilton said.

I looked around at the visitors dressed in their finery, waiting for the doors to open so they could take their seats.

The man soon returned and told us we had five minutes with Mae, but that Gilbert was busy.

"I'll wait here for you," Hamilton said as he stood against the wall.

"I can't believe it," Lottie whispered.

I smiled. At least Lottie would not have to pretend to be an eager fan.

We nervously followed the member of staff who helped us navigate the maze-like hallways of the music hall. I was surprised at the peeling paint on the walls as we made our way to Mae's dressing room. The dated décor was contrasted with the modern style of the foyer, which must have been given a recent makeover. I'd read that the building itself had been built in the late eighteen hundreds.

The staff member showed us to the dressing room and then turned and left.

I took a deep breath, exchanged a glance with Lottie, then knocked on the door.

"Come in," Mae called out to us.

Lottie's eyes opened wide as I took her hand. The door creaked as I opened it, revealing a cramped yet colourful space. Bright shimmering fabrics hung from the walls – a multitude of glamorous costumes were draped over covered boxes and exotic props were crammed in the corners. Mae sat in front of a vanity mirror applying make-up.

She gestured for us to take a seat without turning. "Ah, my admirers! I'm so pleased to meet you!"

Lottie glanced at me as if she expected me to react negatively to being referred to as an 'admirer'. I gave an inward smile.

Mae continued to apply her stage make-up, which was much heavier than that she had worn the night Coltrane died. She was dressed in an ornate blue dress with sparkling beadwork and her blonde hair was smooth, shining in the light. She waved a hand at us upon which was a huge sapphire ring.

I noted Mae's accent had a distinct edge to it, making it somewhat 'put on'. I guessed it was part of her image and that, in reality, she was born of the working classes. It was heartening to find her talent had been discovered.

'We are so excited for the show tonight," I said. "And thank you for seeing us at this difficult time."

She frowned as she applied her lip colour in the mirror. "Difficult?"

"Forgive me, but someone told me that you sang at Millar's Hotel, the other evening. I hope you were not too distressed by the man that collapsed." I did not mention that I was there. The room was busy – it was unlikely she would have recognised me and she had left before the commotion when the police arrived.

Mae ignored my comment about Coltrane. "I hear you have travelled far?" She continued to stare at her own reflection, having not given us a direct look.

"Yes, we took the train to get here," I said, not actually saying where it was I lived. "I heard your performance was cut short at the hotel because of that unfortunate man's death."

Mae picked up a fan and fluttered it around her face as she pouted at her reflection and ran a single finger over her forehead. "Indeed, unfortunate."

"And with you knowing him so well," I added.

Mae retracted her fan with a snap and turned to stare at me. "Why do you say that?"

I put a hand to my chest. "Someone I know said you were close friends."

"That's a lie." She turned back to her reflection and reopened her fan. "I can't even bring his face to mind." Her accent began to falter and I thought it sounded not dissimilar to Lottie's.

I pulled a newspaper cutting of Coltrane from my bag. "Such a handsome man. Are you sure you did not know him?"

Mae narrowed her eyes at me. "Have we met before?"

"No." I moved the picture closer to her.

Mae stiffened as her gaze rested on Coltrane's picture. She stared for a long moment then turned away. "I don't know him at all, and I need to warm up my voice, so if you don't mind."

"Thank you for letting us in," Lottie said – she was already making for the door.

"It's been lovely to see you," I added.

Mae nodded but said nothing further.

Once outside the room Lottie turned to me. "I think she knew Major Coltrane and is lying."

"So do I. She's a firm suspect on our list. Let's get back to Captain Hamilton and watch the show."

"Thank you, my lady." Lottie lowered her eyes and then looked back up again. "I'm so excited to see it."

Back in the foyer, Hamilton approached us. "Any luck?"

"Mae said she did not know Coltrane, but it was quite clear that she did," I said. "She's a woman with a secret, in my opinion."

"And, from the sounds of it, she's about as posh as me," Lottie said.

"I too thought she was masking an accent," I said.

"Let's watch the show and keep our ears to the ground and see whether we can question Gilbert," Hamilton said.

We took our seats. I sat between Hamilton and Lottie as the variety performance began.

I smiled as Lottie giggled beside me. It appeared as if she was having the best night of her life. It was a great performance and being one of the crowd pleased me. The atmosphere was tangible sitting in the stalls. Every act appeared to be more thrilling than the last, and the audience responded with huge cheers and applause. After the interval, Mae Grey finally took to the stage and the curtain lifted behind her to reveal a small orchestra. There was no doubt that she was the main act of the evening. As she sang, her voice appeared even stronger than it had at Millar's hotel. The last number was a melancholy love song. Emotion oozed from her as she sang about lost love whilst moving gracefully across the stage.

As the piece concluded, Hamilton turned to me. "Her voice fills the entire hall."

"And her presence commands attention," I added, feeling goosebumps on my skin at her haunting tones.

Lottie clapped furiously.

There was a standing ovation from the audience. And as Mae stepped to the edge of the stage to take a bow, Gilbert Barry strode over to her like he owned the place.

"Ah, our second suspect," Hamilton said.

Gilbert shook hands with the conductor before embracing Mae. He stepped forward to address the hall. "Thank you for coming this evening. Mae will be here for another five days, so do come back." He waved at the audience before guiding Mae backstage.

I rose from my seat. "Let's see if we can speak to Mr Gilbert Barry whilst we're here."

CHAPTER 11

*B*ack in the foyer, Hamilton turned to me. "Shall I make another appointment?"

I shook my head. "Let's go to the stage door. We'll catch them as they leave."

"They could be some time, my lady," he said as he followed me to the door. "I would not want you to wait in the chilly evening. Would you like to go back to Millar's with Lottie?"

I turned and laughed. "Not at all. We're in this together."

"Right you are," Hamilton said.

"And as you said earlier, Captain. Three heads are better than one."

I linked my arm with Lottie's, who grinned as she looked about her.

Once outside, we walked the periphery of the music hall until we found the stage door and as we approached, it opened. I stepped back as two people exited. Both wore hats with their heads lowered to hide their faces but I instantly spotted Mae. She wore her distinctive sapphire ring and Gilbert's gait was also recognisable.

Hamilton glanced at me and I nodded, confirming I knew it was them.

"Where do you think they're going?" Lottie whispered.

"Maybe back to the hotel?" Hamilton said as we watched them walk away from us.

"Let's find out," I said as I motioned for Hamilton to follow us.

The three of us tailed the pair through the fairground, leaving an acceptable distance, until Mae and Gilbert left through a side gate policed by a guard.

"They've slipped out," Lottie said.

"Let's hurry to the main exit, we don't want to lose them," Hamilton said.

After meandering through the crowd, we stepped out of the fairground and double backed onto the promenade. To the crowd, Mae and Gilbert were unrecognisable as the famous pair they were. But we spotted them, having noted the overcoats and hats they wore.

Once they had passed us, we followed the pair to the bars which lined a section of the road. The bay had really come alive in the late evening. The night was filled with the sound of jazz music. Mae and Gilbert took a side street and then entered a building a few doors up. Bright lights illuminated the name of the place: *Jake's Jazz Bar*.

"We'll be too conspicuous, the three of us," I said. "Captain, you stay here with Lottie." I could not leave her outside alone.

"I can't let you go in unaccompanied," he replied.

"Nonsense, this is nineteen twenty-four, the modern era. If I'm not back in ten minutes then you can come inside to check on me." I turned before Hamilton could protest and entered the bar.

Once inside, I found it dimly lit and the air thick with smoke. The floor was wooden and off-white and it creaked as I walked on it. There were several tables and chairs dotted throughout, some occupied by couples with faces lit by the candles upon the tables and some by groups of friends enjoying their evening. Most people were fashionably dressed. A man held a curtain open for another to enter a back room and I glimpsed a large table beyond, as men and women played cards. I heard the sound of chips clattering in the centre of the table. It was clear there was much gambling here. On the right of the room was a small stage where a male vocalist was accompanied by a pianist. I wondered what the night would bring if I shared a table in such an establishment with Hamilton. I stopped my daydreaming and scouted the room for Mae and Gilbert.

I soon spotted them at one of the tables near the back of the room, engaged in conversation. I wandered over and took my place at a nearby empty table and sat down. The jazz singer paused to drink from a glass. I could now clearly hear Mae speaking.

"I want to leave, tomorrow," she said.

"You can't, darling," Gilbert said.

Darling? I thought. *Certainly more than mere colleagues.*

"You're contracted for a further five days," he continued. "What's wrong?"

The vocalist announced his next song so I was unable to make out Mae's response. The waiter appeared and took my order of a glass of champagne. As he left the table, I again heard the conversation.

"Our problem has been solved," Gilbert said in a loud voice which reached my ears. "Relax."

I stared at them, hoping to hear more, just as Mae's head swung around and her gaze locked with mine.

She stood up. "Her," Mae said with her arm out ramrod straight, pointing at me. "She's the woman I was telling you about. She's spying on us."

I decided it was time for me to take my leave. I stood up and then hurried outside, feeling guilty about my unpaid drink– although it had not yet been served to my table. As soon as I reached Hamilton and Lottie I said, "Let's go."

"Hey, you."

We turned to the sound of Gilbert's voice.

He pointed at me. "If I see you bothering Miss Grey again, or within one hundred yards of her, there'll be trouble. Do you understand?"

"That's no way to speak to a lady," Hamilton said.

I put my hand on Hamilton's arm, not wishing him to divulge my true identity. "I'm sorry, Mr Barry. I did not mean to impose, it is a mere coincidence that we were in the bar at the same time. I was simply assessing whether the establishment was suitable for my young sister here, and indeed I find it is not." I pointed inside.

"You expect me to believe that?" he said. "After you accused Mae of being associated with that waste of space who died this week?"

I took my chance. "You knew Major Coltrane as well?"

"You, madam, are an extremely rude woman," Gilbert paused. "Neither I nor Mae had any connection at all to that man. Now if you please, I need to get back inside to console her. Good evening." He spun around and left us.

I hooked my arm in both Lottie's and Hamilton's as my heart thumped against my chest and we headed in the direction of the hotel.

"That was scary," Lottie said.

"Indeed," I said, but secretly felt thrilled following the altercation.

"Do you think he could be the killer?" Hamilton asked.

"He's certainly a contender," I said. "Coltrane loved to gamble, maybe that is the connection between him and Gilbert, as Jake's Jazz Bar appears to be a gambling joint. Maybe he was killed over a debt." I shivered. "Let's get back, Prince may be wreaking havoc. We will reconvene at breakfast."

. . .

THE FOLLOWING morning inside my suite, I scratched my dog's ear, feeling guilty for having left him. Once again he had ruined a cushion. "I shall take Prince for his walk this morning, Lottie. I'll return in one hour and we'll meet Captain Hamilton for breakfast at nine, as arranged."

"Are you sure?" Lottie asked.

"Yes, he's distressed after we left him last night and it was unfair of me to scold him. He usually has the run of Ashcombe Hall and the grounds of the estate."

"Are you going to hide the cushion?"

The cushion had been a fancy embroidered one, part of a matching pair.

I shook my head. "No, I will confess to Mr Breckon and offer to pay. We won't be able to leave Prince alone again, other than for a quick half an hour or so."

"I'll tell him if you like?" Lottie said.

"No. Prince is my responsibility. Take time to relax in the bath. There are various salts in there, help yourself." I smiled at her.

"Really?" Lottie beamed back at me. "What if housekeeping come in and tell Mrs Flint?"

"It's really none of her business, but I will place the 'do not disturb' notice on the door as I leave. Come on, boy," I said as I fixed Prince's leash onto his collar.

Once on the ground floor, I passed Mr Breckon's office and stopped as I heard a raised voice and listened.

"I'm sorry, sir, but I do not have the funds," Breckon said in a flustered voice, then paused.

I looked through the crack in the door and saw Breckon on the telephone, looking extremely red-faced.

"I appreciate that and the hotel also has a reputation which needs to be kept maintained." He paused. "Fine, eleven o'clock, this evening at Jake's."

I swiftly moved away as I heard Breckon replace the receiver of the phone. I bent down to pretend I was adjusting Prince's collar as Mr Breckon stormed out of the office. His face was crimson and his eyes bulged. It was clear that events were getting on top of him.

"Is everything all right?" I asked as I stood up.

Prince growled.

"Yes, my lady." He stopped and bowed to me. He blinked as if trying to calm his temper and fixed a false smile upon his face. "Are you going for a morning walk?"

"I am indeed."

He took a deep breath as if composing himself.

I contemplated letting him know about the cushion but decided that this was not the ideal moment.

Breckon nodded at me then continued to the reception without further conversation.

I followed and found that Olive was back at the desk.

"You have customers." Breckon gestured towards a couple walking through the door, following the porter who carried a case.

Olive looked at me and then turned away without smiling. I had no clue as to what I had done to upset the girl and had an awful suspicion that she blamed me for Coltrane's death. *Does she think I'm a killer?* I asked myself.

Breckon turned his back on her and headed for the Seaview Restaurant.

"Welcome to Millar's Hotel," Olive said with exuberance to the new guests.

Where people die in their soup, I thought, deciding to wait while the couple checked into the hotel and to take the opportunity to ask Olive a few questions. I watched her give them information about Branden Bay. She handed them their key and directed them to the lift.

I made my way to the desk but Prince pulled at his leash, keen to escape the hotel to the beach.

"I heard you were unwell?" I said to Olive as I pulled Prince across to the desk.

"A stomach ache. Nothing serious," she said.

"As long as it was not the soup," I said, then realised my joke was in somewhat bad taste.

She scowled at me.

"I can understand what a shock it was, seeing a much-loved client die in such an awful manner..." I trailed off.

Olive sniffed. "I've never seen a dead person before."

"Did you know him very well?" I asked in a gentle tone.

"No more than any of the other staff." Olive moved a hair from her forehead.

"He was a regular then?" I asked.

"Yes," Olive said and cleared her throat. "This was his third visit. He was here only a couple of weeks ago."

"So, did you get to know Major Coltrane at all?" I asked. "Is that why you were upset?"

"Me?" Olive blushed. "No, he just seemed like a friendly man. It was a shock. I'm quite embarrassed by my reaction. But no, I did not know him personally." She forced a smile.

"Is the car ready?" A shrill voice filled the reception. "I have an appointment and don't want to be late."

I turned at the familiar voice to find Mae Grey approaching the reception desk.

Mr Breckon was following her.

"You?" Mae stabbed her finger at me having increased the volume of her voice. "Have you followed me to my hotel? I'm going to report you to the police. What newspaper are you working for? I'm sure your paper is only good for wiping your –"

"Miss Grey," Breckon swiftly interrupted.

She continued to stare at me.

Prince barked.

"And what sort of mongrel is that?" she said, pointing at my dog before turning to Breckon. "I need to check out. This hotel has gone downhill," she said in her 'put on' posh voice.

Breckon's mouth fell wide open, looking to me and then back to Mae as if he had no idea what to do.

Olive came from behind the desk. "I'm so sorry Miss Grey that you wish to leave. Is there anything we can do to convince you to stay? Would you like to take tea with Mr Breckon to discuss this?" She looked to Mr Breckon who appeared speechless.

Mae pointed at me. "I'll stay if you get rid of this harlot and her stinking pet."

Breckon gasped and Olive stood there, stunned.

I was also somewhat speechless. I had never before been spoken to in such a way. Not that I was bothered – I knew I had overstepped the mark by spying on her the previous evening.

Olive turned to me in what appeared to be a genuine concerned reaction. "I'm so sorry, my lady." Then turned back to Mae. "I think there must be a misunderstanding. Lady Ellen is here as our guest, she's on an extended break from Ashcombe Hall, which is being renovated."

Mae stared back at me, blinking. Her mouth fell slightly open and she visibly swallowed. "Lady Ellen of Ashcombe Hall?" she asked in a near whisper as she put a hand to her throat.

I was surprised that Mae Grey had heard of me, I was not particularly well known in London outside of the titled families. I smiled at her in an attempt to diffuse the situation. I had no intention of alienating the woman, indeed I wanted to discover the truth of her association with Coltrane and that required persuasion.

"I'm pleased to be formally introduced." I reached

forward and took Mae's hand. I lowered my voice. "It has been a stressful time for all of us, with poor Major Coltrane's demise. He was a neighbour of mine. Would you like to take tea with me?"

"Please accept my apologies," Mae stuttered as she put a hand to her brow. "I've had a bad week. You know what us theatre types are like." She slapped on a smile. "Drama, drama." She waved her hand in the air. "Maybe another time, as I'm due at the music hall." She gave a short laugh then left through the main door.

"I'm deeply sorry, my lady," Mr Breckon said, having found his voice. "New money often arrives without manners."

I smiled. "Not at all, Mr Breckon. When I arrived, I said I wanted to be treated like everyone else." I laughed. "My dear man, it appears that my wish has come true."

Breckon gave a visible sigh of relief.

I looked through the glass doors as I watched Mae climb into the hotel motorcar. *I wonder where she's really off to?* I thought as the motorcar headed in the opposite direction to the promenade. *Tensions are certainly running high.*

"Is there anything you need, my lady?" Olive asked, being notably more polite under the gaze of her manager.

I leant down and rubbed Prince's back. "No, thank you. My dog is keen for his walk."

I turned to leave and coming through the door ahead of me was Mrs Flint, helping a red faced and dishevelled woman. I realised on closer inspection that the woman was Norma Lloyd, the cook.

"Mrs Flint, you should have brought her through the service entrance," an already flustered Mr Breckon said as he caught me up.

"Norma, they let you out?" Olive called from behind. "Thank goodness, as if you'd poison someone."

Norma pointed at Breckon. "John, I'm here to ask for the day off. I've not slept, the bed was a bench, not more than a foot wide."

"I'm taking her to the kitchen for a bite to eat," Mrs Flint said in a soft voice. "The poor thing is starving. The sooner they bring in a more likely suspect the better," she said, then shot me a look laden with accusation.

"I want to forget this whole horrible experience," Norma said as she broke into a sob.

"Please, Norma, not in front of the guests," Breckon said, throwing me a look.

"I'm not in the mood," she said with a dismissive wave of her hand.

I watched as Mrs Flint helped Norma through the reception area. I had much to tell Hamilton and Lottie over breakfast.

CHAPTER 12

*A*s we took breakfast in the half-filled Seaview Restaurant, Lottie updated the notebook. We sat a good distance from the other guests.

Lottie looked up from the book. "So, we still have Norma Lloyd, John Breckon, Mae Grey, Gilbert Barry and Olive Cox. They all have said they didn't really know Major Coltrane that well and the only person on our list who knew him before was Norma." She frowned. "Is Norma our top suspect?"

I shook my head. "I believe they all knew Coltrane a lot better than they're letting on. Each of them is frightened that they will have the finger pointed at them for his murder so they're denying it."

"I don't blame them," Hamilton said as he cut a piece of bacon. "I know what that feels like. And all of them will be hot under the collar, considering Inspector Stone has an empty cell."

"As far as Mae Grey is concerned, I assume she

knows me through reputation," I said as I cut into a slice of toast topped with scrambled egg. "If she knew Coltrane a lot better than she is letting on, then he may have mentioned me, considering we were neighbours."

"At least young Olive would appear to be over the shock," Hamilton said.

I poured myself a cup of tea. "Does Olive have a boyfriend?" I asked Lottie.

Lottie shrugged. "I don't know her that well, but I can find out."

"Olive is extremely pretty, I'm sure she would have been subjected to Coltrane's attention," I said. "But for now, I wish to focus on Mae. She conveniently swooned after Coltrane's death and was removed from the scene," I said. "She could have smuggled the poison out of the room, believing we may be searched. She left before the police even collected her details so I doubt either of them are on their radar.

"Lady Ellen."

I looked up and my mood instantly dropped.

Inspector Stone stood in the doorway of the Seaview Restaurant with Sergeant Chambers.

Stone approached the table. "Can I have a word, my lady?"

"Inspector, Lady Ellen is eating," Hamilton said. "This is a most inconvenient moment."

I dabbed my lips with a napkin. "If it will not take too long? Where would you like to speak?"

"The manager has offered his office," Stone replied.

Prince growled.

I rose from the table. "I'll be back shortly, I'm sure the inspector will not keep me for too long," I said to Hamilton.

Lottie stroked Prince's head in an effort to calm him. "Be a good boy."

I passed the inspector and made my way to Breckon's office with my head held high. As I reached the room, Breckon was frantically tidying papers from his desk. He dropped a sheet of paper and I picked it up, but he scurried out before I could hand it to him. I looked down at the paper to see it was a bill for an extremely pricey bottle of whisky with Coltrane's name at the top. That would be another unpaid bill Coltrane had left, as well as that for his hotel room and no doubt a hefty bar tab.

"Lady Ellen?"

I looked up to see Stone staring at me. I folded the paper and placed it on the desk.

"You appear to be extremely nosey, my lady," Stone said.

"I prefer the term inquisitive, Inspector. An attribute we no doubt share?"

He huffed as he pulled his notebook from his pocket.

I smiled at him, sweetly. "So, I take it you have ascertained the poison used?"

"It is currently an unknown substance and has been sent to London for testing. But I'm here to ask the questions, not answer them." He huffed again. "I spoke to Edward Jacobs this morning." He looked at his notebook. "'I have never been acquainted with Lady Ellen of Ashcombe Hall' were his exact words."

I frowned. "Edward Jacobs? It's not a familiar name to me." I had no idea what the inspector was getting at.

"The police commissioner?"

"Ah." *Dash it,* I thought. The inspector had checked with him after all. "My apologies," I said with a short laugh. "I must have confused him with another fellow." I frowned as if wracking my brain. "Oh yes, now I have given the matter further thought, I've confused him with a very agreeable man that I met at the Ministry of Defence – a Mr Derek Anderson." I smiled sweetly at Stone but this did nothing to soften his countenance. I could tell he was not convinced I was speaking the truth.

"I will now interview you, fully." He sat up straight.

"Now?" I asked.

"Yes, my lady. Unless you wish to return with me to Branden Bay Police Station?"

I gave another short laugh. "This location is fine, Inspector."

"I understand on the night of the murder you lifted the lid of the tureen containing the soup?"

"I did, it smelled divine. Pea and ham is a favourite of mine."

"And did you deposit any substance into it?"

I sighed. "If you're asking whether I laced the soup with poison, in full view of the cook and hotel manager, then no, of course not."

"So, you laced it in private?"

"I did not put any poison in the soup, whatsoever. Is that clear enough for you, Inspector? And if I had, as you have suggested, Major Coltrane would not have been the only victim."

"When did you meet Major Coltrane?"

"As I said, he was a neighbour. Coltrane must have been fifteen the first time I remember him. I was but five years old. He was fishing in our family lake, which was not permitted. Papa, that is the late Earl of Ashcombe, was awfully angry."

I paused, remembering it quite clearly. It was around the time when Mama was taken ill and later died.

"As an adult, Lady Ellen. When did you first embark on a relationship with Major Coltrane?"

"In my late teens, when he showed me attention after his family had sold a chunk of their land to Papa. I guess he thought an alternative to inheriting the land his parents had sold off was to marry me."

"And you had a relationship with him?"

I sighed. "I fell for his charm and he was, back then, an extremely handsome man." I paused, remembering our relationship. "Coltrane was good to me, I was fond of him." I could not escape the memories of the Albert I had met, when he was a charming man. I took a deep breath. I could see now that he had always known how to reel a woman in, like one of Papa's carp, when he needed something from them. "He was in the forces and appeared to be an upstanding gentleman. We were betrothed some months later."

"And how did the relationship end?"

"He went to London as war broke out. News reached me, via social circles, that Coltrane was having a romantic affair with another woman."

"And she was?"

"A chorus girl. I obviously I called it off."

"How did he react?"

"He ignored me to begin with. Then, a few weeks later, my father passed away and as his only child, with no male heir, he left me the estate. I inherited Ashcombe Hall, the grounds and farmland – at a very young age." I took a deep breath. "I'm extremely fortunate and wealthy. Coltrane returned to Ashcombe, lied to me, and told me that my jealous friends had concocted the story about the affair with the dancing girl. But that was not the case. I had the girl's name."

"And the name of the woman was?"

I frowned, trying to remember it. "Green. Yes, a Miss Green, who danced beautifully, apparently, and stole his heart."

"So you still loved Coltrane?"

I shook my head. "I never was in love with him. I was a young girl, not yet a real woman. Later, when I met Leonard, it was clear to me that what I felt for Coltrane was not love."

"And I take it Leonard was your husband?"

"Yes, we only had two years together, but we packed in a lifetime of love." I felt a lump form in my throat and quickly swallowed it down. I didn't want to show

121

too much emotion to this hard man as he interviewed me – just enough to make me appear human.

"Right, yes… Sorry for your loss," Stone muttered.

I smiled. It was my intention to build a rapport with Stone, to eradicate any notion of his that I was the sort of lady to kill a man.

"And you accused Coltrane of murder? With a love that strong, I can understand what lengths a bereaved woman would go to for revenge."

I pursed my lips. Stone was sucking me in with his questioning. Wondering how to proceed, I took a deep breath. "Since Leonard's death, Major Coltrane continued to pursue my affections. I made it clear to him from the very first moment that I was not interested in him."

"Because you accused him of killing your husband and wished him dead," Stone said as if it was a fact.

"Inspector, I do not appreciate your line of questioning. I have not committed murder. And as much as I despised Major Coltrane I have never wished death upon him."

"You have the biggest motive, Lady Ellen. And I understand that Captain Hamilton is your lover?"

"Absolutely not." I stood up. "I think, Inspector, as I have already suggested, you should concentrate on discovering facts rather than listening to endless gossip. That way you may get a little closer to finding the real killer, instead of harassing me. Now, are you going to arrest me? Or am I free to leave this room of my own accord?" I chastened myself for my outburst.

My anger was surely making me appear guilty and the inspector had won in his quest to unnerve me.

"You're free to leave but you may wish to contact your solicitor, my lady. As soon as I have completed my outstanding lines of inquiry, I will collect you for formal questioning."

I felt nausea settle into the pit of my stomach. Surely this man did not believe I was a cold-blooded killer? A chill coursed through my body as the realisation hit. Not only had Coltrane caused me an enormous amount of stress during his lifetime, but now, post death, he continued to threaten my freedom. Or worse. *Surely, I will not be sent to the gallows?* I thought.

CHAPTER 13

*B*ack at the breakfast table in the orangery, I felt anger mix with my nerves and found I had lost my appetite. The excitement of the investigation had been obliterated by Inspector Stone's accusations.

Hamilton caught the waiter's attention. "Can we have a refill of coffee?" He turned to me. "Lady Ellen, would you like me to order a brandy?"

I shook my head. "No, thank you."

"Was he rude to you?" Lottie asked, her eyes full of concern.

Prince whined and I gladly stroked his head in an effort to calm myself down. "He's a man with a job to do," I said. "But he clearly thinks I murdered Coltrane and suggested that I contact my solicitor." I sighed. "I had better place a call to him."

"Stone likely thinks you and I are in cahoots," Hamilton said.

"He certainly mentioned something like that," I said, too embarrassed to tell Hamilton that the inspector accused us of being lovers.

"I don't like seeing you like this, my lady." Lottie lifted the notebook. "The sooner we interview the rest of the suspects the better."

I forced a smile and patted Lottie's hand. "Don't worry about me, my dear."

A fresh pot of coffee arrived and we remained silent as the waiter poured us each a cup.

I took a sip then placed my cup back on the table. "As we are expediting matters, I would first like to speak to Norma Lloyd, the cook." I picked up a pastry. "I will eat and then write her a note and Lottie, if you could place the message underneath her door, she will hopefully meet us."

After breakfast, we all returned to my suite. Lottie played with Prince whilst Hamilton read the newspaper, checking for any new information about the poisoning. It was, I decided, extremely fortunate that I had such large lodgings and could accommodate my guests. I wrote the note to Norma Lloyd and Lottie delivered it for me.

After only half an hour, there was a knock at the door.

Hamilton stood up and answered it.

"Norma Lloyd to see Lady Ellen," she said.

"This way, Mrs Lloyd." Hamilton welcomed her in. "I hope your stay at the police station was not too harrowing."

Norma was dressed in her cook's uniform and was wringing her hands. "It was awful."

"Relax, Mrs Lloyd," I said. "Do take a seat." I gestured to the settee.

"Would you like a cup of tea?" Lottie asked her in a kindly voice. "We've some in the pot."

"Yes please, Lottie dear, what an awful business."

Lottie poured the tea and added a biscuit to Norma's saucer.

Norma took a sip of tea. "So, there's been a whisper that you're investigating this death. I'm really keen for the killer to be caught as I feel Inspector Stone is sure it was me."

"We're also sure that the inspector thinks it was us." I gestured to myself and Hamilton. "It's just his way. The truth is the man has no clue what happened."

"I told the inspector that if it was in the soup, the major wouldn't be the only one to keel over." She took another gulp of tea. "We assumed it was a heart attack until we saw the newspaper. Never thought he would have been poisoned."

"As you say, my dear, Major Coltrane was not the only person to taste your soup," Hamilton said. "And I must say, I'm extremely impressed with your work."

Norma blushed. "Thank you kindly, Captain. Although whoever it was that done it, they did us all a favour, but don't tell Inspector Stony-Face I said that."

"Not many people were fond of Major Coltrane," I said. "We hear you had a history with the man?"

Norma nodded. "I don't like to speak ill of the dead, but he was rotten – rotten to the very core."

"That's quite refreshing, Mrs Lloyd," I said. "You see, I've been asking everyone if they knew him and they're denying it. At least you're honest."

"I worked for his family briefly, back in Ashcombe." She nodded at me. "And I heard how awful he was to you while I was there. Cavorting with a woman of the night in London."

"Ah, yes, the village gossip," I said, also noticing that the story had become somewhat sensationalised, as the woman in question was a dancer, not a lady of the streets. "I don't recognise you. Were you at the Manor for long?"

"It was merely a few weeks. I'd given up my previous position at the palace, after Mr Lloyd died. The job in Ashcombe looked ideal, and I thought a small family would be better for me to cope with than the work for the royals. Mrs Coltrane was charm itself, telling me it was going to be this great job with her friendly family. It was to be a place for me to live within a homely environment, while my heart healed."

I put my hand to my lips. "I've not sent my condolences to the Coltrane family yet." I realised I really should have done. "They must think me incredibly rude."

"I wouldn't feel too bad about that, my lady. They're a dreadful family. When I got there, I had no assistant in the kitchen, and they expected me to do all of the shopping, lugging it back from the village shops on foot. And to do the cleaning and all. I was like a slave to that wretched family. They expected me up at the crack of dawn to wait for them to get up, whenever they pleased, and then cook them individual breakfasts. I worked for the King and Queen in London and they always made it to breakfast at the same time each morning. The Coltranes thought they were better than bloomin' royalty. And they only wanted me working there because of my employment history, so they could brag to others about having a cook who had worked at the palace." She shook her head. "They lied about my pay and all, it was awful, so I just upped and left. Came back to Branden Bay where I was born and had family. Then got the job here. This hotel has been the best thing to happen to me in years." She wiped her eyes with a handkerchief. "And now it's all gone wrong."

"Did you make any observations of anyone here at the hotel who could have killed Coltrane?" I asked.

"No, not at all." She shook her head.

"I understand he and Mr Breckon had words?" Hamilton asked.

"Mr Breckon? I'm sure he had nothing to do with him. He's an upstanding man. Look, no one liked Major Coltrane, he was rude." She sighed. "The thing is, no one will admit to that now he's dead. If I'd known he'd been murdered, I would've kept me big trap shut too. Maybe I wouldn't have been kept up at the police station for so long."

"Did you see Coltrane speaking to anyone in particular at the hotel?" Hamilton asked.

"Well..." Norma paused.

"It won't go any further," I said, eager to hear what she had to say.

"He did seem a bit sweet on young Olive on reception. She's an odd one that girl," Norma said.

"Olive's a bit young, isn't she?" Lottie said. "For Major Coltrane?" Her eyes were wide open as she raised her eyebrows.

"I saw them arguing the day he died. I didn't tell the police, because that slip of a lass is no killer and I didn't want her interrogated."

"What was said?" Hamilton asked, urging her on.

"Olive was accusing him of having an affection for another woman and I heard one name in particular." She looked into her cup of tea.

"And may I ask whom that was?" I asked in anticipation.

Norma looked up at me. "I'm sorry, my lady, but it was your name. Coltrane of course denied it and said that you were once betrothed but that he called it off."

"What a despicable man," I said. "The engagement was indeed called off, but by myself."

"So, if Olive was angry that he held affection for Lady Ellen, then she must really have had a romantic connection with Major Coltrane," Lottie said in a near whisper, then pulled a face before she wrote the details in my journal.

Norma shook her head. "I don't want to point the finger at no one else – Olive's innocent and she was so upset when he died. That's why I never mentioned it to the police." She heaved herself to standing. "If you would excuse me, I'll be getting back to the kitchen. I said I wanted a day off but all I'm doing is worrying about this whole mess and tossing and turning on me bed. And with it being the hotel's pay day today, I'm going to go out tonight to cheer myself up. I can't do that if I've spent the whole day not working."

"Thank you for coming to see me, Mrs Lloyd. You've been most helpful," I said.

Once Norma had left, Lottie picked up the notebook. "I've made some notes to say Norma hated Coltrane but that it was not the soup, because the kitchen staff finished it off and no one was sick." She flicked the page. "That she used to work for his family who were horrible and that Mr Breckon disliked him."

"Hmm," I said. "Although Norma played it down, and made no comment about Breckon, my instinct is telling me there's something afoot with him. I heard him planning to meet someone this evening at Jake's Jazz Bar. Considering it's payday and gambling goes on in there, I'm suspicious."

Lottie's eyes widened. "Are we going to interview Mr Breckon?"

"I think I would rather we followed him," I said. "We do not want to upset him and find ourselves without accommodation. He is a very guarded man."

"He would be if he's guilty," Hamilton said.

"Are we going to Jake's Jazz Bar?" Lottie asked.

"We can't take Prince with us," I said. "And I don't

think it's safe to take you in there, my dear. It's no place for a young woman."

"I would be honoured to accompany you," Hamilton said to me.

I felt a flutter in my chest at the thought but pushed it aside. There was an investigation to follow. It would not be a romantic rendezvous.

"That will be nice. I'm happy to stay back with Prince." Lottie gave me a coy smile then grinned at Hamilton.

"At least we're down to four suspects," Hamilton said. "I do not believe Norma could have done it."

CHAPTER 14

*H*aving eaten in my room, I met Hamilton in reception. I fought the flutter of excitement which rose to the top as he stood there, smiling at me. I was sure he became more handsome as the days passed.

As I reached him, I saw Breckon at the reception desk helping a line of customers, assisted by Olive.

"Shall we have a drink in the hotel bar?" I asked Hamilton. "It will be some time before a certain person makes their way to town."

"That's an exceedingly good idea," Hamilton said as he offered me his arm. "My lady?"

I took his arm and we went to the bar which I had not yet visited. This room also had floor to ceiling windows and the sun had not yet set, giving the room an orange glow. The bar was circular and had a large array of drinks available. It was busier than the restaurant had been in recent days and people sat in couples and groups, appearing to be in good humour. It looked to be business as usual and one would never have guessed that a man had died in the room next door, just days previously.

A waiter hurried over and took our drink orders. I had planned to steer clear of alcohol as we needed to be alert, but nerves got the better of me and I ordered a small glass of wine. As I watched the waiter walk to the bar, I wondered whether the nerves I felt were to do with finding a killer or that I was spending the evening with Hamilton.

Hamilton began to chitchat about nothing in particular, as if he had sensed my nerves and we talked freely as I described how the land at Ashcombe had developed since he had last been there.

"You have done remarkably well, my lady, considering how many landowners have had to sell."

"Honestly, the motive was not to run a profitable estate. The issue I had was that the men who had stayed at the convalescent home wanted to remain and I was trying to create jobs for them. I've a huge workforce compared to the average, and they're happy to work for a reasonable wage as well."

"Your heart is like no other, my lady," Hamilton said. "And you have an aptitude for business. More so than our new Prime Minister." He shook his head. "MacDonald needs to buck his ideas up. But let's not talk politics." He smiled at me and gazed into my eyes.

I picked up my glass of wine and took a rather large sip, nearly a mouthful.

"And what of the house?" he asked.

"Again, I have a huge workforce, working hard. I'm not modernising the hall, I hold it too close to my heart with the memories of my family. I am merely refreshing the original décor, to be sympathetic with the historic nature of the building."

"That is an exceedingly good idea and I'm sure in the long run it will be for the best to preserve the history of the place," Hamilton said as he looked around the room. "As much as I like the modern style, it lacks the intricate details that can give a place charm."

"I hope you will visit," I blurted out before I thought about what I had said.

"But of course, I would be most honoured."

"It should be only a matter of months until it is complete. Now that the village has many more men we have an awful lot of new babies," I said with a laugh. "I am thinking of building new cottages." I took a deep breath. "Papa bought a huge chunk of land from the Coltranes when they were in financial trouble and that area, which is closer to the village, is ideal for development.

"It sounds to me as if Ashcombe has a thriving community."

I nodded. "It has indeed."

"They owe you so much."

"I don't see it like that myself. I'm the lucky one, fortunate to have eager workers. But I do need to come up with a plan for the future so I can keep them employed."

"Even if they have to leave, you've provided each of those men with not only time to heal but also with work experience and new skills."

I nodded. "Luckily I was also able to find jobs for the lame men." I felt a lump form in my throat. Being away from Ashcombe and seeing the whole project objectively, I felt proud of what we had achieved. "I could not have done it without my long-term loyal staff. It's been very different for them." I decided to change the subject, feeling emotion rising up. I did not want it to get the better of me. "Hamilton," I said. "I've told you all about Ashcombe Hall, now tell me how you're doing?"

"Ah, you want to know why I still carry the stick?" He tapped it as it was perched against the table.

I nodded.

"I plan to give it up. Then as soon as I put it aside, I have another dreadful nightmare. Or will freeze during a situation." He turned to me. "That's what this trip was about. To spend a week stress-free and give the stick up for good, to test the waters so to speak." He smiled at me.

"Oh, dear," I said. "I feel rather guilty, dragging you into all of this mess with Coltrane."

"Not at all, my dear. It's hardly your fault and despite the stress of the police investigation, I must say, I feel thoroughly invigorated."

I laughed and glanced out of the room to see

Breckon hurrying past the entrance. "I think the manager is on his way out."

"Shall we?" Hamilton said as he rose from the table.

We walked to the promenade in silence as we watched the sun setting before us, it appeared to dip into the water, I knew then that I loved spending time with Hamilton. It felt natural and a part of me wished I could once again call him Ernest.

We had kept our distance from Breckon, who was not the fastest walker. He checked his watch as if he was late. Beneath my coat, I wore my most fashionable and daring dress. After all, we were going to a stylish bar, with jazz music and dancing, frequented by The Bright Young Things. I felt not so young myself, but I wanted some of that carefree nature to run off onto me.

As we followed Breckon, we saw him turn at the street upon which Jake's Jazz Bar was situated and watched him walk up the road until he went inside.

"You were right. It's where he's headed. Let's leave it awhile before we go in," Hamilton said.

"I agree. At least we know he's in there. Let's carry on, along the promenade for a little." I breathed in the sea air as I listened to the waves gently hitting then retreating from the shore. "I feel most at ease in this town, even with the investigation. It's so liberating being one of the crowd."

"I can't imagine you ever melting into the crowd," Hamilton said.

I smiled, feeling young again. Hamilton was exceedingly good company and I rather enjoyed his compliments, listening to the tap of his stick as we walked.

He looked over my shoulder and frowned. "I say, isn't that the young girl from reception?"

I turned around to see Olive, walking along the other side of Beach Road. She stopped at a public bar called The Branden Arms and went inside.

"Let's follow," I said.

"That's no place for a lady," Hamilton said. "I popped in there the other day and it's full to the rafters with working men."

"If Olive, a young woman, has gone inside, I'm sure I can."

"You will be too conspicuous in your finery, I will go inside myself," Hamilton said.

I had to concede. This was nothing to do with me being the weaker sex but I had rather dressed up. "I'll wait here then," I said as I stood by the sea wall.

Hamilton made his way across the street, being careful to look out for the motorcars. The town was busy and I guessed it was pay day for a lot of workers. While I watched him, I smiled, realising that try as I might to resist, I was falling for Ernest Hamilton. I shook my head. Such an upstanding man would never cross the line and accept my affections. But that did not stop me dreaming. I watched couples strolling along the promenade, playing out their romances under the gaze of others, seemingly oblivious to the outside world, reminding me of when I had first met Leonard. The innocence, the pure joy of a first love. Real love, not the forced affection I'd had with Major Coltrane. As soon as his face came to mind, I saw the vision of his death. I shuddered. As romantic as this town was, a killer was clearly on the loose.

Ten minutes later, I saw Olive leave the public bar and set off back in the direction of Millar's Hotel. Hamilton soon followed and waved at me as he came out and crossed the road.

"Did you discover anything?" I asked as he reached me.

"She was waiting at the bar when I arrived. I perched myself at the other end and after a while a grim looking brute came down. He was a thick set fellow, with a dark beard wearing a flat cap."

"Did you catch his name?"

"No, but he asked her 'have you got it?' She shook her head and he asked her why not. And told her that if she did not give it back to him, he would go up to Millar's and get it himself."

"It might not be related to the murder," I said. "But keep those words in your head, in case it is, so we can make a note of them when we return."

"I certainly won't forget the look on her face, the young girl was terrified," he said. "I only left after she did."

"She went back in the direction of the hotel," I said. "I think we've left Breckon long enough in Jake's so that he'll not have a clue that we tailed him. Let's head to the bar."

As we reached Jake's Jazz Bar, Hamilton opened the door and we went in.

We were shown to a table by the bar's namesake. Jake was a fashionable fellow in a suit. He had slicked back hair and the thinnest moustache I'd ever seen. With it being the weekend, there was a vibrant atmosphere with a full jazz band on the stage. The room was incredibly smoky and I wondered whether I would be able to spot Breckon through the cloud it created.

"What can I get you?" Jake asked as we sat at a table for two with a candle in the middle and a small vase containing two petite pink roses.

"Two Martinis," Hamilton said choosing for us both. "Is that acceptable?" he asked me.

I nodded at the waiter. "That will be ideal." I glanced around the room as the waiter left our table. "I can't see him, can you?" I asked Hamilton, trying to make it less obvious that I was searching for someone.

A female singer joined the stage and I turned and smiled as a group of young people took to the floor and danced the Charleston. I'd not seen it performed with such skill and energy.

"I don't know how they manage it," I said with a laugh.

"It's a bit too energetic for me," Hamilton said.

I smiled. "If Breckon wasn't here, I'd challenge you. We could take lessons – I saw some advertised at the hotel," I added without thinking and then blushed as the waiter deposited our drinks on the table.

"All I can manage are slow dances," Hamilton said, clearly nervous of his dancing ability. "I have an issue with timing. My mother tried her best to teach me as a lad, hoping I would woo a nice girl at the local dance."

As if the band had heard Hamilton's mention of a slow dance, they began a ballad.

I took a rather large gulp of my drink and smiled at Hamilton. "Well?" After all, I had planned to dance while in Branden Bay, away from the hall, in such a bar as this.

Hamilton propped his stick against his chair and held his hand out to me. I took it and we took to the floor and moved with the music as if we had been dancing together forever. I felt so free and found that Hamilton was clearly putting himself down as I was sure he could feel the beat of the music. I clean forgot about Coltrane and his death. For a while, I simply enjoyed the moment in Hamilton's arms.

As we came off the floor, Hamilton nodded to a booth in the corner and frowned as he looked over my head. Then spoke into my ear. "Well, I never."

I glanced to the far corner where I spotted Breckon holding hands across the table with a woman.

"Who is she?" Hamilton asked.

"It's our cook," I said as Norma put her head back and laughed.

"So it is," Hamilton said.

I turned back to Hamilton. "I do believe we are back to five suspects."

"Indeed. Mrs Lloyd failed to mention she was

romancing Mr Breckon. She would no doubt lie for him and lead us in the wrong direction by pointing the finger at Olive."

"Do you think they know we're here?" I asked as we retook our seats.

"By the look in the chap's eyes, it seems he's too absorbed with Mrs Lloyd to notice anyone else."

"They could be working together," I said. "After all, they both had the opportunity to lace Coltrane's soup." I took a sip of my Martini.

"But you said the exchange between him and the person he was talking to on the phone was slightly aggressive," Hamilton said.

"It was and certainly not the way a man would speak to a…sweetheart. This is most curious."

The waiter approached Breckon and spoke to him.

Breckon nodded and held out his hand to Norma. She took it and they both picked up their drinks and took them to the back of the room. As the curtain to the concealed room was opened, I saw someone else who was on our radar.

"Gilbert Barry," Hamilton and I said in unison.

"That's who he's meeting," I said. "He was probably waiting for his game to end. It seems there are many gamblers connected to the hotel."

"And more people that Coltrane may have owed money to," Hamilton said. "Or who owed him."

I lifted up my Martini. "Let's enjoy our drinks. We have much to think about."

After three Martinis, we took a slow walk back to

the hotel. Breckon was probably doing quite well in the card game as he had not reappeared and neither had Gilbert, although a couple of other men had come out with downcast expressions. With it being late, there were fewer people on the street and it was a starry night. The air was crisp and fresh, carrying with it the aroma of seaweed and hints of the warm summer days yet to come. I looked around at the lights twinkling from buildings nearby and smiled. It had been a truly blissful evening.

As we neared the hotel, Hamilton bowed to me. "Thank you for a wonderful time and I look forward to our breakfast debrief tomorrow morning."

He waited for me to go up in the lift, alone.

I opened the door to the suite slowly, not wanting to wake Lottie, but when I opened the door, it was to find her pacing the floor with a letter clutched in her hand. She rushed up to me.

"My lady, it's Sebastian. He's coming across tomorrow to see me. Can you believe it? Would it be rude of me to ask for some time off, so soon, to see him?" she asked.

"Calm down," I said. "Tell me exactly what's happening."

Lottie passed over the letter which I read as I raised my eyebrows. The young man was visiting a cousin at Gosford Hall on the outskirts of Bristol and would take the train to Branden Bay. I feared that nothing good would come from Lottie cavorting with a man so many steps up the social ladder that she was. He may as well reside in heaven he was so far out of her reach. A young man who might not have respectable intentions. As Coltrane had once told me, after his affair in London, a man needs to sow his wild oats. I did not want Lottie to be used in such a way.

"I shall accompany you as your chaperone," I said.

Lottie blinked but did not say a word.

"Remember, you are officially betrothed to Joseph Flint. It could be extremely awkward and detrimental to your reputation. I know Sebastian, we have met, although he may not remember me. However, a scandal is less likely if I accompany you." I would also make sure her dignity was not compromised.

"He wants us to go to the fairground," she said with bright eyes.

"Then we shall also bring Hamilton. It's late, now get to bed, Lottie. We have much to discuss tomorrow at breakfast." I had the feeling that Lottie was too excited for sleep.

CHAPTER 15

*L*ottie could barely sit still at breakfast.

"Are you feeling quite well, my dear?" Hamilton asked her.

I looked around to see if anyone else was in earshot. "Lottie is meeting Sebastian, The Earl of Garthorn, the childhood sweetheart we spoke of. The young man is travelling here today."

Hamilton raised his eyebrows. "I see."

Lottie nodded, her face flushed, clearly realising that Hamilton did not approve.

Prince nuzzled Lottie's hand for a stroke.

"You and I will be chaperoning," I said to Hamilton as I placed a slice of toast on my plate.

"I understand why," he said, clearly sharing my reservations.

"He wishes to visit the fairground and is meeting us there. We are going to enjoy the rides and then take tea at the pier tea rooms before he departs for home."

"Shall we update the notebook with last night's observations?" Hamilton asked Lottie, clearly changing the subject as Lottie was blushing fiercely.

"Yes, Captain," Lottie said and we updated her on what we had observed, impressing on Lottie that the liaison between Mr Breckon and Mrs Lloyd would need to be kept quiet from the other members of staff.

THE SUN SHONE BRIGHTLY, providing us with a warm summer's day and I put up my parasol as we waited for young Sebastian on the promenade.

Hamilton had Prince by the leash.

I watched as Lottie nervously waited for the young man who held her heart. As much as I wished for social lines to be crossed, I did not wish Lottie to suffer a broken heart. I knew that this young man had been a big part of her childhood and I planned to observe them together, believing that the connection could possibly be more akin to family. If she had played with him as a child, she may really see him as a sibling.

I spotted the young man, with the same dark hair as his mother, striding towards us. He was much taller than I remembered and he sped up as soon as he saw Lottie. He rushed up to her, held out his hand for her to take and then lifted her up as she squealed. She smiled brightly as he lowered her. Sebastian dressed in a smart cream suit, with a blue cravat – it was clear he had made an effort for this meeting. Lottie had borrowed a dress from me, one which was modern yet not too short.

"Lottie, you look beautiful," he said as we approached.

"I didn't think you would recognise me," she said.

"I see a vision of you in my mind every day." He gazed at her.

"I can't believe you're really here," she said.

My heart swelled as I watched them and realised this was far from a brotherly-sisterly love. Indeed, the pair had much romantic affection for each other.

After our introductions, Hamilton and I gave them distance for privacy, but not too much in case they were spotted. As they walked around the stalls and stands they laughed. Prince sniffed the air, licking his lips whenever food was in the vicinity. Hamilton had to pull at his leash a few times to prevent him eating fallen food. The fairground bustled with people of all ages, flocking to buy treats from the stands. There were a few stalls selling handmade trinkets such as beaded necklaces, colourful embroidered scarves and painted clay figures. We took a ride on the carousel and I laughed as Sebastian nearly slipped off. I felt as if the youthful innocence of the pair was rubbing off on me.

Hamilton was less relaxed and had not ridden any rides, keeping his hand on Prince's leash and his eyes upon the young couple. I smiled at him. He was acting very much as the protective elder brother towards Lottie and, whilst I wished he would relax and enjoy the fairground, I admired him for his caring nature.

Once we had seen everything the fairground had to offer, we gave Prince a run on the sands before moving to the pier. We took a slow walk along the wooden boards and Lottie and Sebastian stopped, leaning against the railings. I watched as they pointed to small boats bobbing in the bay then Lottie tugged on Sebastian's arm in amusement as she pointed out a seagull attempting to steal food from a man's hand as he ate.

Hamilton and I stopped to watch a young woman juggle flaming torches and further along two clowns performed acrobatics. We finally reached the tea rooms at the end of the pier, just before the landing where the boats disembarked. I approached Lottie and Sebastian. I had given them enough time alone. I wanted to know how serious this young man was about continuing a romance with his childhood sweetheart.

"Let's take a table and have tea together," I said. "I'd love to hear your news, Sebastian."

After we were shown to a table, Prince settled down underneath it.

"I must say you have grown into a fine young man," I said. "And you clearly have much affection for Lottie."

"I'm going to do all I can to prevent her marrying Joseph Flint. And thank you for looking out for her, she has told me how you have helped by delaying the wedding with the position you have given her as your assistant."

"I hope your intentions are honourable," Hamilton said to Sebastian, not mincing his words.

I smiled at his approach.

"Of course, Captain. Once I leave university, where I'll be reading English Literature, I shall find myself paid employment."

"Really?" I said, not hiding my shock. What on earth would the Marquis of Bandberry think of his son living the life of a commoner!

Sebastian took Lottie's hand. "I intend to have Lottie in my life and be a working man."

Although I hoped this indeed would be the case, for Lottie's sake. I knew how much sway big families like his had. I felt saddened and guessed Sebastian's well-meaning romantic notion would be quashed by his parents' wishes and may well dissipate as he matured and the realities of life hit home.

"I've had a wonderful day, Lady Ellen." He glanced at his watch. "The last train back to Bristol is in an hour. I would have loved to visit the music hall."

"We went the other day," Lottie said. "We saw Mae Grey."

Sebastian sat back in his seat. "I've a friend whose older brother is absolutely obsessed with her. He's seen her many times in London." He laughed. "His father works for MI5 and ordered a background check on her to dash poor Bunty's dreams of a union." He lowered his voice. "It seems she was an illegitimate child. But don't repeat it." He leaned back. "It would not bother me. Marriage is a human ritual, creating a child is a fact of nature."

"I won't tell anyone," Lottie said. "I have to keep all sorts of secrets." She gave me a sideways look.

"Mae has done well for herself," I said. "If she had a humble upbringing."

"Yes, good for her," Hamilton said. "I heard she's made great wealth from her performances."

"It took a while for them to track her past, because she changed her name of course," Sebastian said. "It used to be Maude Green."

I felt my jaw drop and I stopped breathing. The world around me changed from a hubbub to a buzzing noise. I pulled my fan from my bag and fluttered it before my face.

"Are you well, my dear?" Hamilton said. "The colour has drained from your cheeks."

I swallowed. Maude Green was a name etched into my mind forever because Maude Green was the dancing girl that Coltrane had romanced whilst engaged to me. One thing I knew for sure: Mae Grey had known Major Albert Coltrane intimately.

CHAPTER 16

$\mathscr{J}$ had chosen to have an early night following the revelation of the day before, keeping it to myself as I was still processing the matter. I'd had many restless dreams of Mae and Coltrane and had been unable to enjoy a deep sleep until the early hours of the morning.

At just gone eight o'clock, I was awakened by the sound of banging coming from the door of my suite. I bolted upright, hearing Prince frantically barking. This was followed by shouting. I could make out Lottie's voice and that of a woman. I rose out of bed and grabbed my housecoat.

Yanking open my bedroom door, I found Lottie holding Prince back, with Mrs Flint in the corner of the room as if he had trapped her there.

"Get that animal away from me," Mrs Flint shouted.

"What on earth is going on?" I demanded as I tied the cord of my housecoat. 'Prince, heel."

Prince turned and sloped to my side with his head bowed, realising I was not at all happy with him. I put my hand down to stroke his head to reassure him. After all, he was only protecting Lottie. "I can assure you, Mrs Flint, that Prince is not a dangerous dog."

"I'm sorry, my lady, I was bitten as a child." Mrs Flint had her arms across her chest.

"What brings you to my suite at such an hour?" I asked.

"I came to speak to Charlotte."

Lottie turned and looked at me, her eyes red and her cheeks streaked with tears.

"Can I asked what the issue is?" I asked.

"It's a private matter," Flint said.

"Lottie?" I asked.

Lottie licked her lips. "Mrs Flint said someone saw me with a young man, unchaperoned yesterday at the fairground."

"Mrs Flint, you should not listen to idle gossip," I said.

"Lottie is betrothed and it's not decent for her to be seen cavorting with another young man," Mrs Flint said.

"Your facts are wrong. Lottie was with me at the fairground, she was not unchaperoned. It was crowded and yes, she may have been seen talking to all manner of individuals. The fairground is a busy place."

"Joseph is anxious about the upcoming wedding, especially as it's been delayed," Mrs Flint said. "Due to her temporary position with yourself, my lady. So I have come to give message that Joseph wishes to take Lottie out."

"Well, that is most fortunate as we are going to the music hall this evening and I can chaperone the pair," I said.

"Well, I was planning to go myself..." Mrs Flint trailed off.

I nodded at Lottie whilst Mrs Flint was looking the other way.

"Of course, that would be nice," Lottie said. "Joseph loves music, he told me so when we last met. And he loves the piano."

"That's agreed then," I said. "Please meet us in the hotel reception at seven-thirty this evening." I did not relish an evening spent in her company, however I did not want to leave Lottie alone with the pair.

"Well, yes." Mrs Flint nodded at me and left the room.

Lottie plonked herself on the settee as soon as Mrs Flint had left. "I don't want to go out with Joseph."

"You owe an explanation to the young man. If you're meeting Sebastian, then you must call it off with Joseph as soon as possible. I feel uneasy about being dishonest to Mrs Flint and her son, so the sooner you end this engagement the better."

"I guess you're right. I need to tell Joe, it's just not right for us to be wed."

"Exactly, and I want to interview Mae Grey, so I will ask Hamilton to mind Prince for me while we go. I don't trust anyone else with Prince and I can't let him destroy any more cushions."

"So you've decided to focus on Mae Grey?"

I sighed. "I will explain it all at breakfast. Could you please call through to the captain and ask him to meet us in the Seaview Restaurant at nine?"

"ARE YOU WELL, LADY ELLEN?" Hamilton asked, as we began our light breakfast of tea and pastries.

"Yes. I had a shock yesterday, a revelation I could not mention in front of Sebastian."

"What happened?" Lottie asked with her pen poised.

"I know for sure that Mae Grey had a strong link to Major Coltrane," I said.

"And how did you come by this knowledge?" Coltrane asked.

"Sebastian told us she was called Maude Green – that was the name of the lover Coltrane took, while he was betrothed to me."

Lottie gasped. "No wonder she was off with you."

I shook my head. "Quite the opposite. Mae had no knowledge of whom I was until she heard my name here, at Millar's. Her countenance changed immediately when she discovered my identity. She was as pleasant as can be. I thought it odd and now wonder how I didn't notice the similarity between Mae and Maude and Grey and Green. It's an obvious choice for a stage name."

"So, knowing who you are," Hamilton said. "She doesn't want to rock the boat. And for us to delve into her background and discover who she really is."

"It would be more than a slight on her character," I said. "It would put her in the frame as a murderer."

"And she might be scared you will be angry with her," Lottie added. "For having relations with your fiancé."

"Not only that, but she could well have poisoned his soup. She was sat close to the bowl whilst we were arguing with the blighter," Hamilton said. "Would you like me to escort you to the police station so we can pass this information on to Inspector Stone?"

I gave a short laugh. "Absolutely not. The inspector is a buffoon, he will probably accuse me of making it up, alert Mae and then she could possibly skip town. No, I will speak to her myself. I'm off to the music hall with Lottie and Mrs Flint's son this evening."

Lottie looked up and then back to the notebook.

"I will leave Lottie to have a somewhat awkward discussion with Joseph Flint, while I meet Mae, or should I say – Maude."

"I would feel better if I could be there to protect you, my lady. The woman is possibly a murderer."

"I need someone to stay with Prince," I said. "Would you be so kind to sit him for me?"

"My lady, I will take him with me and wait outside the music hall."

I smiled at him. "Thank you." I took a deep breath. "I will be pleased when this whole nasty business has been resolved, as I find it most disagreeable having to think every day about Major Albert Coltrane."

"You look beautiful, Lottie," I said as she gazed at her reflection in the free-standing mirror, wearing another of my own gowns.

"I don't want to look beautiful." She turned to face me with a frown. "I don't want him to like me."

I sighed. "It's not a crime to be an attractive young woman. Now, come along, until you see him you'll be unable to call off the engagement."

When we reached the hotel reception, Hamilton approached us and took Prince's leash from me. Prince wagged his tail so much his hind was moving.

"Ready to go for a walk, boy?" he asked him.

Prince barked.

"I rather think, Hamilton, that you may have to go on ahead of us and give the dog a good run on the beach. We'll meet you on the prom, by the billboard, in half an hour?"

He looked at his watch. "See you at seven forty-five," he said.

Lottie touched my arm. "There he is, my lady." She nodded towards a lanky young man wringing a hat in his hands. "He's early."

I smiled. "The poor thing looks utterly terrified."

"With a mother like Mrs Flint, anyone would be," Lottie said in a low voice.

"At least his mother isn't with him," I said.

We approached the young man.

He gave me an awkward and far too low bow with his hat in hand. "My lady, I am honoured to meet you." He stretched back to standing and held his hat to his chest, as his face flushed red.

I waved a hand dismissively. "Please, call me Lady Ellen.

"Unfortunately, Mother can't make it. She's unwell."

"Oh dear," I said, yet felt relieved. "Not something serious, I hope?"

"I don't think so. She hasn't made it home, but Father says it's a stomach bug."

"I hope she gets better soon," Lottie said with a smile.

"Shall we?" I gestured towards the front door. "Lottie, why don't you walk with Joseph?"

Lottie gave him a small smile. "How are the rest of your family?" she asked him.

I walked ahead, listening to the stilted conversation between the two, mainly about their families' health and the weather. I picked up quite quickly that young Joseph was as much interested in Lottie as she was in him – quite frankly, not at all.

As we neared the prom, I motioned for them to sit on seats beneath a cast iron canopy. "Let's sit and wait for Hamilton."

Lottie pointed to the sands. "I can see them." She turned to Joseph. "See the dog with the shiny red fur, that's the dog I'm looking after."

Joseph appeared to relax as he watched Hamilton throw a stick for Prince.

I smiled as the young man calmed down. "Have you been to Branden Bay Music Hall before?"

"No, my lady, I've always wanted to but..."

"Your mother didn't let you go alone?" I asked.

He nodded. "I only turned eighteen last month. She must be really upset at missing it, she loves Gilbert Barry," he said with a laugh. "Dad gets jealous about it."

"Tonight will be a real joy, I'm sure," I said. "We loved the show when we saw it earlier in the week. I've booked a box."

Joseph took in a sharp breath. "I erm..." He blushed.

"Joseph, it's my treat. If that is what you were worried about?" I saw him visibly relax. "You can spend the money you were going to use on the tickets on confectionery."

He smiled at me with big blue eyes. He was, I thought, sweet and I hoped I was correct in my belief that he did not hold too much affection for Lottie, considering she was about to end their association.

We waited as Prince dragged Hamilton towards us.

Hamilton stamped his feet to free loose sand. "That was rather exhilarating." His eyes shone and I was pleased that I saw a difference in him every day that passed. Whilst he still held his stick, it was placed over his arm.

"Let's head for the music hall," I said.

"I will wait at the gate to the fairground," Hamilton said.

"Really, Captain Hamilton, there is no need. The show is on for two full hours."

"On second thoughts, I will sit in The Branden Arms. When I was in there before, it appeared that dogs were welcome. I'll come for you at ten." He turned to Joseph. "If there are any problems, come and get me there." He pointed to the public house situated on Beach Road.

Joseph nodded his head. "Yes, Captain." He lifted his hand as if about to salute him, then dropped his arm in embarrassment.

I suppressed a laugh. I was sure that I had never before met such an awkward young man.

When we reached the music hall, we filed in with everyone else and were shown to our box.

Joseph's face lit up as he watched the show. "This is wonderful. I can't wait to see Mae Grey."

Whilst I would not wish illness on anyone, I was pleased Mrs Flint had not joined us.

Mae arrived on stage to close the first half and began to sing. Joseph's eyes shone with tears and when Mae stopped singing, he clapped ferociously.

I stared at the woman, now seeing her as the dancing girl Coltrane had spent time with when he was betrothed to me. At the time, I had imagined her to be a brazen woman, but there was a fragility about Mae, and, behind her eyes, a passion in her heart. It was likely that Coltrane had led her on and who was I to judge her previous choice of career?

I stood up. "I'm going to see Mae."

"Can I come?" Joseph asked, his earlier shyness seemingly evaporated.

"It's a delicate matter," I said.

"Please," he near whispered.

I looked at Lottie then back at Joseph. "All right, come with me, say hello and then return to this box." With a murderer on the loose, I wanted them to stay safe.

CHAPTER 17

On the ground floor of the music hall, I waited until no eyes were upon us and then ushered Lottie and Joseph through the door marked 'private'. This time I knew exactly where I was headed.

Joseph and Lottie whispered excitedly behind me as we navigated the dim lit corridors until we arrived at Mae's dressing room. I took a deep breath and then knocked.

"Who is it?" Mae called out.

"Lady Ellen of Ashcombe."

It went quiet but I could hear movement inside and a whisper.

Mae answered the door with a nervous smile. "Lady Ellen, what a nice surprise, I didn't know you were in tonight."

"I have an extremely eager fan here," I said gesturing to Joseph.

Mae pulled a silk dressing gown over her dress and

came out of her room. "Let's go through here. My dressing room is too cluttered."

I heard movement from inside and wondered who was in there. Clearly someone Mae did not want me to notice.

"Miss Grey," Joseph whispered as we followed her. "You're amazing."

She turned her head and smiled at him then beckoned for us to follow her. Two doors up, we found ourselves in a large room with a piano and a few scattered tables and chairs.

"This is where we practice," she said.

"Joseph plays piano, don't you," Lottie said.

"Help yourself," Mae said gesturing across the room, then turned to me. "Shall we talk over there?" She pointed to a table in the corner.

Lottie and Joseph headed towards the baby grand.

Mae sat down and offered me a cigarette. "Smoke?"

"No, thank you," I said, "I tried once and made a fool of myself spluttering until I was really quite ill." I laughed. "My housekeeper has never liked the aroma and every time I am offered a smoke, I see her disapproving face in my mind." I shook my head. "I lost my real mother as a child and Dawkins has always been a matriarch figure in my life. Even though it is me who employs her, I am not sure I will ever quash her air of authority."

"Does she have family of her own?"

I shook my head. "She's a spinster and devoted her

life to the hall, and keeping me in line. I fear I may have disappointed her a few times."

Mae attached a cigarette to a black holder. "I'm sure she's really proud of you." Mae lit her cigarette as Joseph began to play the piano.

With the music loud enough to mask our voices, I decided to change the line of conversation dramatically. "You said you did not know Major Albert Coltrane."

Mae's eyes darted to me, looking extra large with the thick stage make-up. "You know?"

I nodded. "You are Maude Green."

She took a long drag of her cigarette and then blew the smoke upwards. "Albert Coltrane left me. I did not know he was betrothed to you."

"I'm not here to pass judgement," I said.

"He told me he loved me. That we would be together forever." She looked me in the eye. "I never killed him, my lady, even though I hated the man. He took something from me, my heart, my innocence, and then left me…"

"Penniless?" I asked.

"He left me with more than that…"

"Yes?" I urged her on.

She sighed. "He left me with child."

I did not know what to say. I had certainly not been expecting her to say that.

"Obviously I tell you this hoping for your silence on the matter. But I need you to know, as you can surely see that I would not kill my daughter's father." She took another long drag on her cigarette. "It was a shock."

I let the fact seep into my mind, then softened my voice. "I had no idea you were a mother. Or indeed that Coltrane was a father."

"And that's the way I want to keep it. It certainly won't go with my stage image. Gilbert said..." She took another drag of her cigarette and blew it away from me then turned her head. "I'm only telling you so that you know I didn't poison Albert, as much as I wanted him to leave me alone."

"Where is the child?" I asked.

Mae looked away. "She was adopted. And is very happy, comfortable and loved with a decent family."

"So Coltrane never took on his responsibility and left you in that predicament?" No wonder Mae was less than impressed to find Coltrane staying at Millar's Hotel.

Mae looked down. "When I told Albert I was pregnant, he gave me the address of a woman who could make it all go away." She looked up at me with a sheen of moisture forming across her eyes. "He said he'd paid for everything and all I had to do was to turn up. But I was too scared." She shook her head. "A friend of mine – she died that way."

"And what did Coltrane say when you kept the baby?"

"I never told him because we never spoke again. Then I found out from a friend that he'd been engaged to you all along. I felt dirty and used."

"Then after the war you reinvented yourself as Mae Grey?"

She gave a short laugh. "Albert didn't even realise Mae Grey was the Maude Green he used to know, even though he had seen my picture. It was not until he saw our show here in Branden Bay, two weeks ago, that the penny dropped."

"Did he try to reconcile with you?"

She nodded. "I didn't want him to find out he had a daughter and possibly ruin her life, when she thinks her parents are other people."

I thought how sad it was that the little girl did not know who her real mother was. A lump formed in my throat thinking of how proud and excited the little girl would be if she knew that her real mother was a star. "Surely he would never have found out?"

"I guess not, but I wasn't thinking straight. As soon as he came backstage to see me, I felt dirty. I wanted nothing to do with him."

"Did he pester you?" I asked.

She stood and gave a theatrical gesture with her arm. "He said he loved me. Huh! More like he wanted some of my money." She took another drag of her cigarette and then stubbed it out on an ashtray in the centre of the table. "I do quite well for myself these days."

I smiled. "You should feel rightly proud of yourself. And I'm sorry for what he put you through." I also felt guilty about the image I'd held of what Maude Green was like. A lush, dancing for male pleasure.

Mae sat down again. "Albert said unless I spent some time alone with him, he would tell the world that I was a common dancing girl or worse. I can't tell the police that, they'll think I had something to do with his death and then everything will be out in the open." She stared at me. "I don't want to be Maude again."

"So do you have any idea who could have poisoned his soup? You were seated close by."

"I was doing my best to look away from his table and kept my eyes focused on Gilbert as we spoke. Although I did see that young girl on reception at his table. I saw her huddled with him a few times at the reception desk, giggling." She raised her eyebrows. "I think you and I can guess what was afoot there." She shook her head. "It appears Albert Coltrane got older but the age of his new conquests remained the same."

I felt sick, hearing Albert's voice in my head. *A chap needs to sow his wild oats.* And thought of Olive, so young. No wonder the girl reacted the way she did. We remained quiet for a moment, both turning our heads to the piano as Joseph began a new tune and Lottie started singing a classic musical hall number.

"They're really good," Mae said with a laugh and stood up. The song appeared to wash away her melancholy mood. It was clear that music had saved Maude Green and did more for her than simply transforming her into Mae Grey.

I followed her to the piano as we watched Joseph's hands moving deftly across the keys.

The door burst open and Gilbert Barry appeared. "You can hear that from the stage!"

Joseph immediately stopped, leaving an echo of his last notes bouncing off the walls.

"S...so...sorry," Joseph stuttered.

Lottie bit her lip and shot a frightened look at me and I thought she was about to burst into tears.

"It's my fault," Mae said putting her hand up. "I said he could play."

"It doesn't matter, my dear." Gilbert's eyes appeared to light up, not dissimilar to the way Mae's had. "I just wanted to see who was playing." He strode over to the piano. "What's your name, lad?"

"Joseph F... Flint. I.. I'm –"

"Who taught you?" Gilbert demanded.

"My Grandfather. I played on his piano from as soon as I could get up on the piano stool." He looked at the keys. "When he went, I inherited his piano and played whenever I could. But during the war, mother chopped it up for firewood when things were bad."

"Have you played with anyone?"

"At school, I played the hymns and stayed behind for hours with the music books. And I worked out how to play tunes I heard." He looked up at Gilbert with more confidence, as if he was the first person to ever ask him about what was clearly a passion of his. "I play at The Branden Arms, across the road, when the lads ask me to. That's how I know this tune."

"And how old are you?"

"Eighteen, sir."

"Any commitments?"

Joseph shot a look at Lottie.

She shook her head and widened her eyes. "No, he hasn't."

Joseph slowly turned back to Gilbert. "No, sir."

"Excellent. I'm tired of playing the accompaniment for Mae." He raised a hand theatrically in the air. "I'm an actor." He laughed. "You have a job, pay is five pounds a week. Board, keep and clothing are included."

Joseph opened his mouth as if he could not find the words.

I stepped forward and put a hand upon his shoulder. "You come alive at the piano, Joseph. I think it's an amazing opportunity."

He looked at Lottie. "But…"

Lottie shook her head. "I'm not ready for that sort of thing and my heart…is engaged elsewhere." She bit her lip.

Joseph grinned from ear to ear and turned back to Gilbert. "When do I start?"

"Can you read music?" Gilbert asked.

He nodded.

"In that case – tonight. Come along." Gilbert led Joseph away.

"Lottie, we will have to get back to our seats. We won't want to miss this." I turned to Mae. "Thank you for confiding in me. I really appreciate it and I'll not breathe a word." I would, of course, be updating both Hamilton and Lottie on the matter. But it didn't feel like they really counted as breaking my promise.

"Thank you for understanding, my lady. Under the circumstances, with the history of the matter."

"Mae," Gilbert called through the doorway.

"I'd better get changed." She turned and left the room, looking a lot brighter than I had seen her yet.

As I watched her go, I knew in my heart that Mae Grey was no killer.

CHAPTER 18

e asked to take a light breakfast in the orangery. I wanted privacy away from the other guests. Hamilton was yet to join me and Lottie was battling the weather in the gardens whilst Prince had his comfort break. The rain poured down in torrents and could be heard drumming on the top of the orangery roof. I watched the droplets of water bounce and zigzag as they raced in a frantic slalom until they eventually pooled in the metal edged window frames. Finally, enough momentum built for the water to overflow in rivulets on the collective downward journey. As a child, I had spent many hours watching raindrops upon windows.

I glanced around the room which was devoid of guests, The remaining customers willing to take a chance on the hotel food had their breakfast in the Seaview Restaurant, but I wanted privacy and not to be overheard when I explained Mae's history to Lottie and Hamilton. Whilst I had updated them on the parts of our conversation relating to Olive, I had not divulged that Mae had birthed Coltrane's child. I looked to the entrance as Lottie entered the room with Prince on his leash. She had removed her coat, which I expected was dripping wet and drying somewhere else. Stray tendrils from her tied-back hair were stuck to her head.

I peered at Prince to check his fur, suddenly worried he would shake and spray the orangery with water, but he was not sodden.

"Thank you so much," I said. "Have you dried him?"

Lottie nodded. "Olive fetched me a towel."

Prince gave a short bark and sniffed the table, as if in anticipation of food. Hamilton strode in with a broad smile upon his face. Prince trotted over to him for a stroke. He had clearly taken to Hamilton.

Hamilton took a place opposite me and Lottie sat beside me. I brought them up to date with what I had learned about Mae and Lottie wrote in the notebook. I told her to ensure we did not let the book get into the wrong hands. We sat in silence for a while as Hamilton and Lottie digested the information I had given them. We did not want to discuss it at length in a public place. After a while, Lottie broke the silence.

"I wonder what Mrs Flint is going to say about Joseph and me calling the engagement off?"

"Hopefully she will be pleased he has a new career," Hamilton said.

"It's better than working in the quarry," Lottie said.

Hamilton nodded in agreement.

"And it's his life and his decision," I added.

Lottie sighed. "I hope Mrs Flint doesn't shout at me."

Hamilton placed his newspaper on the empty fourth seat at our table. "She can hardly blame you."

"Norma said she's still poorly today," Lottie said. "She's stopped being sick so they've taken her back home. She'd got all dressed up for the show yesterday and came here to show Norma her outfit, then got poorly. And I mean really poorly. Norma said at one point she thought they were going to have to call the doctor! She had fish for tea, maybe it was off."

"Whilst I feel sorry for her, it was a blessing for Joseph," I said. "He may not have been given the oppor- tunity with Gilbert if he'd been shackled to his mother all evening."

"And surely she can't be that upset, now that her son's employed by Gilbert Barry, with her being his biggest fan," Hamilton said.

We stopped our discussions as our continental-style breakfast was brought to our table. We ate in silence for a while and I pondered over our suspects.

I dabbed my mouth with a napkin then placed it upon the table beside me. "I would like to speak to Olive Cox, as soon as possible."

"I agree," Hamilton said. "We have two people now who have pointed the finger at her. Norma Lloyd and Mae Grey. Not forgetting that I saw her talking to that unsavoury character in The Branden Arms. I looked out for the chap yesterday evening, but there was no sign of him. And when I asked the barmaid if I could speak to the landlord, she told me the pub was owned by a woman, not a man. A widow called Mrs Kerr."

"So, how are we to get Olive to speak to us?" Lottie asked. looking through the doorway to the reception.

"I shall simply call her over." I stood up and walked to the reception desk.

Olive gave me a weak smile as I approached. "Can I help you, my lady?"

"Is it possible for you to join us for a moment?" I gestured towards the orangery.

"I shouldn't really leave the reception," she said.

"You can see the desk from our table," I said with a smile.

"Very well, my lady." She walked from behind the desk and followed me into the orangery.

"Sit down, my dear," Hamilton said to her, lifting his newspaper from the chair.

She did as she was told and I smiled, taking my seat.

"As you know, the police had me in at the station and we rather fear they believe I had something to do with Major Coltrane's demise," Hamilton said.

"I, too, have been subjected to their accusations," I added.

"So, we would like to ask you some questions," Lottie said.

Olive shifted in her seat. "Why me? I don't see what you think I would know about it."

"We understand that you had dealings with Major Coltrane," I said in a soft voice.

"Dealings?" Olive asked and I watched her visibly gulp.

"I understand there was some form of affection between you two?" I added.

"A couple of people have suggested to us that there was," Lottie said.

Olive gulped and tears formed in her eyes. "Am I in trouble?"

"Don't worry, my dear," Hamilton said. "We are just trying to build a picture of his last movements so we can find who did this horrendous thing."

"I see." She bit her lip.

"Did you see anything suspicious?" I asked.

"No," Olive said, a bit too quickly, as she shifted in her seat.

"So, you and Coltrane were having a romantic affair?" I asked in a quiet voice. "You were ever so upset when he died."

Olive's chin trembled.

Hamilton shot a look at me. I could tell his over-gentlemanly nature was making it uncomfortable for him to watch Olive in distress.

"I know personally how convincing Major Albert Coltrane could be," I said. "I too had a romantic affair with him when I was young."

Olive nodded her head. "He said that I was like no other girl he had met and that he was going to marry me once he had sorted out some business." She looked up. "He said he was coming into some money and that he wanted to take me to meet his parents."

I raised my eyebrows. I guessed that maybe Coltrane was calling in a gambling debt, had a dodgy deal or was blackmailing someone. Coltrane had certainly not worked for any financial remuneration since his exit from the army. Or he was simply stringing young Olive along.

"Then I saw him speaking to you and I was worried he was leading me up the garden path, to do his dirty work," Olive said.

"What dirty work would that be?" Hamilton enquired.

"He liked doing deals and had deliveries." She looked at her hands and then up again. "But don't tell Mr Beckon, he can get frightening when he loses his temper."

"So did you challenge Major Coltrane?" I said.

"I asked him if he still held a candle for you, my lady. But he said I was being a silly girl and I was still the only one for him." She looked down again. "Then he died. I was so shocked and upset, I thought my life was about to change."

"What deals and deliveries did you help him with?" Lottie asked her.

Olive shrugged. "He just asked me to do things."

"Like what?" I asked.

"Errands. Nothing specific." She looked towards the reception, as if willing a customer to arrive. "I was upset but life goes on." She looked me in the eye. "You have to understand, I'd never kill anyone, especially not a man I thought I was going to get married to. A man who would give me a good life and a family."

"Thank you, my dear, for being so honest," Hamilton said bringing the awkward conversation to a close.

I agreed that it was time to end it. Olive was clearly not going to volunteer any further information but my senses told me she was holding something back.

Lottie looked up from the notebook and then shut it.

"Before you go," I said. "I noticed that Mr Breckon appeared to have issues with Major Coltrane."

Olive looked around her, then remained silent.

"It would really help us if you have any information you could share," I said.

"We're all potential suspects, as far as the police are concerned," Hamilton said. "Your name may come up when the police interview others, some of whom have mentioned you to us. So, it's important we find the real killer, otherwise we may be blamed ourselves."

Olive's face flushed red again and she sniffed.

I placed a hand on hers. "Did Mr Breckon owe Major Coltrane money?"

Olive nodded.

"You've been most helpful," I said.

"Is everything all right here?" Mr Breckon asked as he entered the room.

Olive stood up.

"We were asking Olive about places we could visit

in the surrounding areas, seeing as we'll be staying for three months."

He stared at Olive as she scurried back to the reception desk.

"Mrs Flint has called and is asking for you, Miss Penny, to visit her at home. If you could give her some time?" Mr Breckon said to Lottie. "And Norma has asked if you could take some of her chicken soup, which will hopefully improve Ina's health. We can't afford to lose any more staff." He gave me a hard stare. I felt he had regretted allowing Lottie to become my assistant.

Lottie exchanged a glance with me.

Prince barked as Breckon left the room.

"It's going to be about Joseph, she's going to go mad at me," Lottie said.

"Calm down," I said. "You're a grown woman. I always feel it's better to meet these things head on." I stood up. "Come along, Lottie." I glanced at Hamilton. "Could you mind Prince again? I'll order extra coffee for you."

"Of course," he replied.

I pointed to the notebook which Lottie had placed on the table. "And feel free to look through the notebook to see if anything stands out and to add any details we have gleaned from Olive."

We left as soon as the weather had changed from torrential rain to a drizzle. Lottie had tears in her eyes as we exited the hotel. She carried a small tureen of soup. Mrs Flint lived close by, only one hundred yards away.

"Calm down, my dear. Why do you allow this woman to have such a hold over you?" I asked.

As we approached the house we heard Mrs Flint wailing. I took a deep breath.

A woman looking remarkably like Mrs Flint answered the door. "Pleased to meet you. I'm Ina's sister," she said by way of introduction.

"Mrs Flint appears to be in distress," I said.

"That's because her Joseph has just left."

"There she is," Mrs Flint stood up as we entered the small and dark sitting room. "You shamed my boy." She pointed at Lottie.

"Mrs Flint, please be seated," I said as she wavered before plonking herself back in the armchair. Her eyes were sunken with puffy bags underneath.

"She's still a bit delirious," her sister said in a low voice. "But she's much better. By all accounts, the poor thing was retching all night at the hotel and couldn't even make it home until eight this morning!"

"She called off the engagement and Joe plans to run off with the circus," Mrs Flint said with a sob.

"He's not with the circus, Mrs Flint," I said. Clearly Flint had only heard part of the story before Joseph could explain properly. "He's travelling with Gilbert Barry's Theatre Company."

Mrs Flint stopped rocking and looked up. "Gilbert?" she said with a whisper then turned her head to the corner of the room. On the wall was a picture of her idol, smiling. Below that a table, upon which was placed two glasses, a small bottle of eau de toilette, a scrap book with his name on and a folded tissue. I felt somewhat queasy, hoping it did not contain toenail clippings.

Her sister whispered to me: "Ina's a little obsessed."

"It's an amazing opportunity," I said.

"I'm really proud of him," Lottie added. "Even if we aren't…"

Mrs Flint's sister frowned. "So Joe's going to be helping them put on shows?"

"More than that," I said, smiling at Mrs Flint. "He'll be on stage playing the piano for Mae Grey instead of Gilbert. Mr Barry said he wants to focus on his acting."

"Ina, you should be proud." Her sister walked over to her and placed a hand on her shoulder.

"Did Joseph not say?" Lottie asked.

Mrs Flint sat speechless, the expression on her face slowly changing from anger to wonder. Then she burst into tears. "My boy's going to be famous and I shouted at him before he could explain." She stood up. "I have to see him." She struggled for a moment and then fell back into her seat.

Her sister helped her to standing. "You need some proper food and a sleep, Ina. Let's get you to the kitchen and that soup down you, then I'll help you to bed." She looked up. "Then I'll find young Joseph and ask him to pop back and see you."

. . .

ONCE LOTTIE and I were back at Millar's, we found Hamilton and Prince still in the orangery.

Hamilton looked up. "How did it go?"

"Mrs Flint is still suffering from the after effects of her stomach bug. But once we explained that Joseph is working for Gilbert Barry, and hadn't run off with the circus, she appeared over the moon." I shook my head. "She has a shrine at her house for Mr Barry on her drinks table." I pushed the vision of the tissue paper, holding what I suspected was toenails, from my mind. Nevertheless, I sat down and added the shrine contents to the notebook.

"So, Captain." I lifted the notebook when I had finished. "Have you come to any conclusion?"

"I think we have a few contenders, but we need to find out what the deal is with Gilbert Barry. Does he know that Mae had Coltrane's child?" he said.

"Or was Coltrane blackmailing him over his relationship with Mae? I would not put it past Coltrane."

"I overheard Mr Barry at reception ten minutes ago," Hamilton said. "He's taking elevenses with cream cakes in this very orangery, because today is his birthday."

I turned to Lottie. "Do you want to take Prince for a walk now the weather has taken a turn for the better?"

"Yes, my lady. He's certainly ready for it."

Prince stood up having heard the word 'walk' and spun around in excitement.

Lottie giggled as she took the leash and led him out of the room.

179

Hamilton and I remained silent for a while as we sat in the orangery and watched a few people come and go. My mind was jumbled. It seemed that all the suspects had secrets, all of them had a reason to kill Major Albert Coltrane – and a part of me did not blame them. If it was not for the fact that Inspector Stone had made myself and Hamilton prime suspects, I would have let the matter lie. Norma Lloyd was right, whoever had killed him had done us all a favour.

I glanced out to the gardens, where iron tables and chairs were placed. They had been painted white and I watched as a waiter wiped them down, the sun glistening on the pools of water he sought to clear. The hotel was indeed the perfect place to spend my three months away from Ashcombe. It was a shame that death had blighted my stay.

We both looked up as Mae entered with Gilbert and we smiled at them.

"A curious pair," Hamilton whispered to me.

"Indeed, I do not believe they are romantically connected," I whispered back. "I understand from the entertainment press that he is her mentor, that he launched her career."

I stood up and approached their table. "I hear there is much to celebrate."

Gilbert and Mae exchanged a look and Mae nodded. "Indeed, it's Gilbert's birthday."

"I'm having a big party this evening at the music hall, if you both would like to join us?"

Mae had clearly told Gilbert who I was and, as he

was being friendly, I guessed she had explained I was no threat.

"That's most kind," I said. "We would love to accept your invitation."

As their food was brought to the table, I excused myself.

CHAPTER 19

*L*ottie was happy to sit with Prince whilst myself and Hamilton attended Gilbert's birthday party. I left her reading through the pile of letters she had received from Sebastian. The young man had taken to posting her one every single day. I hoped he was not playing with her affections. Surely a union between two people with such different backgrounds was doomed? I thought of Hamilton as I descended in the lift and shook away any romantic notion of him. We too were from different worlds. I realised that I had been letting my heart run away with itself and I had to rein it in.

Once I reached the reception, Hamilton was waiting for me and smiled as I approached him. "As always, you look extremely beautiful, Lady Ellen."

"Thank you. And you also look smart yourself, Captain."

He held out his arm for me to take, the other holding his stick. "I have ordered us a car, my lady."

"For that I am truly grateful." As we passed Breckon's office, we heard him speaking to Olive.

"I don't want that type here, do you understand? It could be difficult for us. The last thing I want is that crook on my case."

Olive came out of the room looking flustered. "The car is waiting out front for you, my lady," she said.

Once we were seated in the hotel motorcar, Hamilton turned to me. "I wonder what was going on back there between Breckon and young Olive?"

"I don't know," I said. "Did you see her wipe a tear from her eye? The girl appears to be under immense pressure."

"I can't help thinking it has something to do with that brute I saw her with in The Branden Arms. We really need to find out who he is."

"I could try talking to the girl, just the two of us, but I fear she will not be forthcoming. Behind her eyes, I see something she's holding back."

"I agree, the young girl was petrified."

We soon arrived at the fairground, which was quiet since Branden Bay Music Hall was closed on a Monday evening. Gilbert's party was being held in the bar, by invitation only. After leaving our coats at the cloakroom, we entered the bar. Joseph was tinkling away at the piano in the corner of the room on a small, raised platform used as a mini stage. He appeared transformed from the nervous young man I had met previously.

"Lady Ellen and Captain Hamilton," Gilbert said as he greeted us with extra warmth than I was used to from him. He had clearly been drinking. "I must say you two make a handsome couple."

I blushed. "And is Mrs Barry here?" I asked, changing the subject.

He shook his head. "It's too far for her to travel from Yorkshire and she's minding our youngest daughter."

I was surprised to hear of a child. I did not see Gilbert as a family man – surely he was unlikely to see much of his family, with all the travelling he was doing on the tour. "It must be hard, being away from your family so much."

He nodded. "I may not be home much, but I'd do anything for them. Anything."

Mae came over at that point.

Gilbert put his arm around her. "I love my girls." Gilbert kissed her on the cheek.

Mae looked embarrassed. "Gilbert, I think you've had too much whisky."

Gilbert stepped back. "And so I should, I'm half a century today! Now let's dance." He dragged Mae off.

"What an odd situation," Hamilton said. "Praising his wife and family, and then cavorting with Mae on the dance floor."

"Indeed," I said as I watched many couples now dancing to the jazz piece Joseph was playing. I smiled at Gilbert's attempt at the Charleston. Mae was excellent at it, flicking her legs and not missing a beat as she mastered the swivel. Her dance training was evident. I had to admire her advancement in society. Gilbert had clearly seen talent when he had set eyes upon her.

"It's exhilarating to be amongst such an enthusiastic crowd," I said to Hamilton.

"Joseph has impressive skills on the ivories," Hamilton said as Joseph ended the lively number and everyone applauded wildly. "I don't even recognise the lad."

Gilbert was now on the small stage and raised a glass. "My latest discovery," he called out and motioned for Joseph to stand up as everyone gave a round of applause.

Gilbert stepped off the platform and gestured to Mae. "But this is my best ever find." He put an arm around her waist and kissed her on the cheek.

Mae looked directly at me with a concerned look upon her face.

I turned to Hamilton. "There's more to learn about those two."

"As in?"

"I've no idea, but it would be most helpful if you could engage Miss Grey in conversation whilst I speak to Mr Barry. As he's inebriated, this is an ideal opportunity to find the truth of the matter."

Gilbert walked towards the bar and I headed after him, leaving Hamilton to engage Mae in conversation.

"Whisky on the rocks," Gilbert said to the barman as I reached his side.

I watched as the barman poured whisky for him over ice.

"That looks nice," I said. "Especially having ice at this time of year."

"They have an ice house here in Branden Bay," Gilbert said. "It's up by the castle. They ship it in over the winter months and it lasts all year round. That's why I love this town. I can't abide whisky without it. We have an ice box at home, you know. The wife calls me Jack Frost," he said, then descended into laughter.

"I have to say, you've totally brought Joseph out of himself," I said as the barman passed him his drink.

"Thanks for bringing him to me," he said. His eyes were glassy and his face flushed.

"I can see you care for your finds, like Mae," I said.

"The day Mae arrived she changed our world." He smiled, a distant look in his eyes.

"At least she doesn't have the likes of Major Coltrane to upset her anymore," I said.

Gilbert frowned. "That man was a parasite on society. I've never met such a selfish fellow in my entire life." He turned to me and lifted his glass. "Do you know, whenever pouring whisky, the man dealt himself a full glass, and his guest only half? A despicable, selfish fellow." He took a gulp of his drink. "Didn't fool me though." He chuckled.

I looked over at Mae and she shot me a worried look.

"Did he owe you money?" I asked, trying to get to the point before we were interrupted.

Gilbert nodded. "Not a large amount. I'm not the sort of chap to gamble money I cannot afford to lose."

"So Coltrane had a gambling habit?"

"Exactly. I play for fun. He had the habit. It was the principle of the matter. He needed to pay his dues. Live up to his responsibility for once in his life."

I had the impression that Gilbert was well aware that Coltrane had left Mae in the family way.

"I'd like to toast the person that killed him." Gilbert lifted his glass, then took another gulp of his drink, the ice jangling against the tumbler. "I admit, in my youth I made mistakes." He ran a hand over his slicked hair. "I didn't want to face up to my responsibilities, but eventually a man has to…" He shook his head. "I doubt Coltrane ever would have." Gilbert began to mumble, as if he was talking to himself. He straightened up. "But I had no motive to kill the man. He owed me money which I'll never get back. I'd have more chance of that if he was still alive." Maybe Mae had also told Gilbert I was trying to find out who had poisoned Coltrane.

"Gilbert," Mae said, interrupting as she arrived at the bar with Hamilton. "I think you should switch to coffee."

He laughed and turned back to me. "This is what I mean, true friends and family care about their fellow human beings. Coltrane did not have a grain of that in his entire body. It was all about him."

"I think," Mae said, "it's time to go back to the hotel."

"I can arrange a cab," Hamilton offered.

"I've already arranged our transport and Gilbert will have to say a few goodbyes," Mae said.

There was a sudden change of music as a huge cake was wheeled in with a mass of flickering candles atop, nearly lighting up the room. I'd never seen anything like it. Mae took Gilbert by the arm and led him to the cake as the room broke into collective singing as Joseph played 'Happy Birthday'.

"I think we should leave now and return to Lottie and Prince," I said. "I want to clear my head and add to the notebook. It's a pleasant evening, let's take drinks on the balcony of my suite."

"Did you retrieve any information from Gilbert?" Hamilton asked as we left the bar area.

"I learned that he loves whisky over ice," I said with a laugh. "He clearly wanted to make a point to me, that he had no motive to kill Coltrane, but at the same time, I felt he was holding something back."

"Something that could incriminate him?" Hamilton asked.

"Maybe."

"And why is his wife absent from his fiftieth birthday party?"

"She's looking after their youngest daughter," I said.

Our conversation was interrupted by a collective cheer as Gilbert blew out his candles. We stopped to applaud, then made our way through the crowd to the exit.

WHEN WE REACHED BEACH ROAD, Hamilton hailed a horse-drawn carriage. He took my hand and helped me climb onto the open carriage and I smiled at him, turning away as I sat down, reminding myself this was not a romantic rendezvous. It was an investigation. The promenade was illuminated by gas lamps which gave the street a warm glow. The clip-clop of the horses' hooves created a gentle rhythm as I calmed my jumbled mind. The carriage took us past the bustling pier before turning onto the road which took us up the hill to Millar's Hotel. The horseman pulled up outside the grand entrance and both Hamilton and I stepped down. I looked back at the twinkling lights of Branden Bay and, with a deep breath of fresh sea air, turned and made my way inside. I felt a different person to the woman I'd been at Ashcombe Hall.

"I'm looking forward to going over everything we have," I said to Hamilton. "I need it to click into place."

When we reached my suite, Prince barked.

Lottie looked up and yawned. "I fell asleep on the settee. Would you like me to go to the kitchens and fetch refreshments?"

"I've already put in a request with the night porter for coffee. We need to stay awake for a little longer, I want to go over everything."

"I can't wait to hear about the party," Lottie said.

There was a knock at the door and Lottie opened it as the porter brought the coffee in on a tray. At our request, he carried it out to the balcony and placed it on the table.

"I have information about Gilbert," I said once the porter had left. "He said that Coltrane was a selfish man and alluded to him not taking on his responsibilities."

"So, you think Gilbert knows all about him leaving Mae when she was with child?"

"I believe so. Even though she wants no one to know about the child, it would appear he was aware of her history. And that adds an additional motive, other than him owing him money."

"To silence him and not ruin Mae's reputation and the success of his travelling show," Hamilton said.

"Exactly," I said.

"And he's very close to Mae. With the drink flowing, he even kissed her on the cheek," Hamilton said.

"And Mae was embarrassed," I added. "As if she would prefer him not to be so tactile."

"Maybe Coltrane threatened to tell Gilbert's wife about how close he is to Mae?" Lottie said making notes in the book.

I sighed. "He seems such a charming man. When I quizzed him about the fact his wife could not make it, he said she was at home with their youngest daughter."

Lottie frowned. "I read about it in the newspaper when they started a family. But I thought they only had one child."

"As Mrs Flint is an admirer of Gilbert, I'm sure she will know all of the details," Hamilton said.

"Let's ask her tomorrow when she will hopefully be back to full health," I added. "I still need to speak again to Norma Lloyd, considering she's clearly a lot closer to Mr Breckon that we realised." I sighed. "There's still more we need to learn before we can discover how Coltrane died."

Lottie pulled a face. "I can't believe Norma and Mr Breckon are... You know."

I laughed. "It's not only the young that fall in love." I looked over to Hamilton, who held my gaze then quickly looked away. I continued. "Gilbert insisted that he had no motive to kill Coltrane, who owed him money which he will now never get back."

"And what about Mae?" Lottie asked.

"Her whole career could be damaged if she was exposed," Hamilton said. "Society can be somewhat judgemental."

"So, your next step is to speak to Mrs Flint about Gilbert and then ask Norma about Mr Breckon?" Hamilton asked.

I nodded, stifling a yawn. "I'm so tired, I'm not confident I will make breakfast. I'll walk Prince first thing and see you both here, on the balcony if the weather is good, for elevenses."

Hamilton stood up. "It's been a most pleasant evening, Lady Ellen." He wished us goodnight and left.

"I think Captain Hamilton has a soft spot for you,

my lady," Lottie said as the door closed behind Hamilton.

"Nonsense."

"What's wrong with his leg?" she asked.

"I'm sure the captain is a proud man and would not want us discussing him in such a way." I didn't think it was my place to tell Lottie that his affliction was shell shock. I knew Hamilton viewed it as a weakness.

"I still think he likes you," she said.

"I think you should calm your internal gossip, Lottie. You have romance on your mind, due to young Sebastian's visit."

She smiled. "I hope he can come and visit us again soon."

CHAPTER 20

$\mathcal{R}$ather than sleeping in, I rose early the next morning and left Lottie in her bedroom, taking Prince for his promised walk. My dog wagged his tail. I knew he loved it more when I walked him. It had been a twice daily event for so much of his life. I felt guilty that I had delegated the morning walk to Lottie. With all the extra food provided by the hotel, I was also keen to take some exercise myself.

As I reached the ground floor, the reception area was quiet. Olive was red-faced at the desk and a man was leaning over and speaking to her. I pulled Prince's leash tight and inched closer so that I could eavesdrop.

"I told you not to come here again," Olive said.

"No one tells me what to do," the man growled.

"I checked his room, I can't find it, it must have been thrown away," Olive said.

"I don't want this coming back on me, do you hear?" The man spoke in an extremely threatening voice.

"I've told no one. And I don't even know where it is. No one has mentioned it."

"So you say. Just keep it that way, I don't want no peelers on my case." He lifted her chin with a thick finger. "You don't want to lose those pretty looks now, do you? And it won't be just you that suffers – remember, I know who your father is."

I heard myself gasp without intending to and, whilst the pair may have missed my reaction, Prince barked and they both turned around. The man stared at me. I was in little doubt that he knew I had been eavesdropping on the conversation.

I pulled at Prince's leash as he growled at the man. "Nice day for a morning stroll, sorry to interrupt," I said as I approached the desk. The man was wearing a flat cap covering a lot of his face, with a dark beard and he resembled the description Hamilton had given me of the man he saw Olive speaking to in The Branden Arms. I gave an involuntary gulp. This was an extremely threatening man.

I turned to Olive. "My morning paper was not delivered."

"I'll see what I can do, my lady," she said in a quiet voice.

The man left without saying farewell.

Olive had tears in her eyes.

"Are you well?" I asked now the man had left the property.

She nodded without speaking.

"Is it something you would like to talk about?"

She shook her head vigorously. "I'll get your news-paper sent up."

I made for the door, realising Olive would not speak to me on the matter, and having heard how threatening the man had been, I could understand why.

Once outside, I looked down the hill and saw the man making his way to the promenade. "Come along Prince, let's see where he goes."

I sped up and was grateful for my flat shoes. The man turned at the promenade and went left. He had a limp so was not going at a fast pace. Now out of the man's sight, I ran along with Prince to reach the promenade.

We caught up as he was not far ahead, but kept our distance, not wishing him to spot us. I was somewhat conspicuous with my red-haired dog. I saw him stop at The Branden Arms and walk inside.

"Bit early for drinking," I said to Prince.

Prince growled.

As we passed the pub, I saw that there was a closed sign on the door, although a shadow was created across the window as someone passed it. I pulled at Prince's leash as he growled then we crossed the road to the promenade. I decided to speak to Olive, once she had calmed down.

We enjoyed a long walk which blew away the cobwebs but I could not get the unpleasant man from my thoughts. I decided to pick up a bone for Prince and headed for the butcher. I walked up the High Street as some of the shops catering for tourists were now opening. The cafés were already alive with visitors taking breakfast.

"Lady Ellen," the butcher said as I arrived. "I have put the perfect bone aside for Prince.

My dog barked and the butcher laughed. "Your dog has bags of personality."

I stroked Prince's head and the butcher passed the bone over to me, wrapped in paper.

"It's on the house," he said.

"I have something to ask you," I said.

"How may I help?"

"I saw a man earlier, wearing a brown coat and a flat cap. He had a dark beard and he looked quite fearsome. Does that sound like anyone you know?"

The butcher's expression changed. "It does and it is also someone I would recommend you forget."

"And what is his name?"

"As I said, my lady. It's not a name I would want to repeat but, to be safe, I would keep away from him." He lowered his voice. "He's as bad as he looks."

I bade him farewell and was struck by the concern in his voice when he told me to 'take care.' But I was still determined to discover who this man was and intended to bring his presence at the hotel to the attention of the police.

Back at the hotel, Olive still appeared shaken.

"This came for you, my lady." Her hand shook as she passed me a note.

"Olive, I'm always here if you need someone to talk to."

"Thank you, my lady."

I took the note and went to my room. I was sure Prince would like a sleep after his long walk.

As I entered the suite, Lottie pointed to the note in my hand. "Who's that from?" Her voice was full of excitement.

I laughed. "It's for me, so not a note to you from Sebastian." As I opened it, the smile slid from my face.

Mind your own business,

else you are next.

"Who's it from?" Lottie asked standing up.

"It's not signed." I passed it to her with a shaking hand.

"My lady." She put a hand to her mouth,

"I'll call downstairs." I picked up the receiver and dialled for reception.

"Olive Cox, can I help you?"

"It's Lady Ellen. Where did the note come from which you just passed me?"

"I found it on the reception desk, my lady."

I hesitated. Olive's voice had been shaky. I decided to question her further. "Who was the man you were speaking to earlier?"

"Which man?"

"The one with the beard and flat cap." I knew Olive was well aware to whom I was referring.

"I don't know, my lady. Please don't say anything."

I could hear the fear in her voice so decided to end the call.

"What did she say?" Lottie asked.

"She didn't, but I have a good idea who the note was from," I said. "Olive was speaking to a rough-looking man in reception and he threatened her and looked remarkably like the brute Hamilton saw her with in The Branden Arms."

"Do you think she's mixed up in something?"

"I certainly do."

"And it's linked to the death?"

I nodded.

"If he has threatened you... We should tell the police."

I sighed. "I agree. This man has killer written all over him, the police need to know. But I'm in two minds as I heard him threaten Olive and her family – speaking to the police may put her in jeopardy."

"We could ask Norma about him," Lottie said. "I asked her if we could speak to her today and she suggested we meet her in the kitchen. She's the only one there this morning. The others are on errands."

We soon entered the kitchen, having left Prince asleep.

"There's tea there," Norma pointed to a large urn. "Lottie, pour some for you and her ladyship."

I sat down. "I understand you and Mr Breckon are very close friends, but you kept this from us?"

"That man's been like a rock to me, having lost my husband. But we're not supposed to have relationships in the hotel. Me and John were childhood sweethearts. It seemed natural when we got together."

"He owed money to Major Coltrane," I said.

"I told John not to play him at cards. The man cheated him, I know he did. Then he kept demanding things. He ordered a bottle of expensive whisky the day he died and had no intention of paying for it, telling John to take it off his debt. The man was a menace."

I was still convinced there was something more sinister afoot. "I saw Olive today speaking to an unsavoury fellow at the reception desk. She appeared very frightened of him."

Norma frowned. "What did he look like?"

"Stocky, with a flat cap and a full dark beard. He was also spotted in The Branden Arms."

Norma groaned. "Sounds like Simon Crow. A nasty piece of work. He's a can-do man. Any job you have, he can do it." She shuddered. "Rumours are he got a taste for killing in the war." She stared at me. "You don't think he killed Coltrane, do you?"

"I don't know," I said. "Do you?"

"He would be a contender, but don't accuse him unless there's strong evidence. He'll slip through the grip of the police. Mark my words, he'll come for you if they don't lock him up." She sighed. "I pity Olive if she's crossed him."

"Did Breckon go to Coltrane's room the evening he died then?"

"Yes, to deliver his whisky," Norma said. "But Coltrane took it to Gilbert's room. I saw him with my own eyes when I was on the third floor, delivering your dog food."

We were interrupted as Mrs Flint breezed in.

"Good morning," she said in a sing-song voice, as if she was a totally new woman.

"Ina, you look so much better. I thought you was a goner the other night."

"So did I, never been that bad before. At least it wasn't catching."

"Good morning, Mrs Flint," I said. "Can I ask you a couple of questions about Gilbert Barry?" I asked.

"I heard you're doing some sort of amateur investigation, my lady. But I can assure you he's an upstanding man." Her mouth returned to the straight line I had become used to.

"Indeed, I understand he's an extremely good and loving father," I said.

"Ah yes," Mrs Flint sat down and helped herself to a cup of tea. "I've newspaper cuttings in my scrap book."

"You and your scrap book," Norma said with a chuckle.

"I was so pleased for them, being blessed with a child. You know when you idolise someone, it's as if they're part of your family when good news hits. And, well, now my Joseph is sort of part of their family." She gave such a broad smile, it was as if Mrs Flint had transformed into a new person. "Gilbert is so handsome. I saw him on stage in London. Then after the war, when he discovered Miss Grey, I saw him with her again. I cannot tell you how excited I was to hear he was staying here, at Millar's."

"So, his children?" I asked.

"Just the one. She's called Emma and lives in Yorkshire, where they're from. They were blessed later in life. I guess he was so busy. The little girl looks so much like him, with her dark hair."

"And how old is she?"

"Ooh, I'd say she must be about eight."

I had a suspicion about the child but kept it to myself. "So, he has no other children?"

"No."

Gilbert's words echoed in my mind. *My wife is looking after our youngest daughter.* At last the fog in my mind was clearing.

CHAPTER 21

*L*ater, I poured tea as we sat on my balcony and read through the notebook.

"I'd like to take a look at Mrs Flint's scrap book," I said, writing a note on the page. Remembering her shrine, I felt some things were falling into place. I also wrote down my other conclusions, about Mae and Gilbert's relationship.

Lottie gawped at me. "Do you have an idea who did it?"

"I'm so close. But I feel I have a major piece of information missing. I'll let you know where I am."

"Yes, do," Hamilton said.

I took a deep breath. "For starters, I believe this Simon Crow character supplied the poison. Olive collected it, either knowingly or unknowingly, and then passed it to the person who had murder in mind. But there is still something missing. How on earth did the poison get into his soup?"

"I think it could be any of them," Hamilton said. "Most of them had access to his soup bowl whilst he was at your table, my lady. Olive's role was to pass the poison to them. Although she doesn't appear to have a close connection to any of the suspects, they could be distancing themselves from her on purpose so not to raise attention to their joint plan. The poor girl has certainly been led astray, that's for sure." He sighed.

"Or blackmailed into it," I said as my instinct told me she was far from evil. "But I think I know the connection between –"

I was interrupted by a knock at the door.

Lottie answered it, then rushed inside and returned to the balcony with a wild look upon her face. Behind her stood Inspector Stone and Sergeant Chambers, backed by two further policeman, filling my suite.

Lottie grabbed hold of Prince's collar and took him to the small bedroom as he barked.

"Lady Ellen of Ashcombe Hall," Inspector Stone said. "I wish to question you about the murder of Major Albert Coltrane." He stared at me.

"Inspector, I was just about to call on you. I believe I have the answers."

He narrowed his eyes. "I'm here to search your hotel room. Ryan, Jones." He gestured at the officers to hunt through my belongings. "Chambers, escort the suspects to the Seaview Restaurant."

"This is ridiculous, do you not want to know what I have to say?" I said. "I know who supplied the poison, if you'd care to listen?"

Stone laughed. "Now that doesn't surprise me!"

"Put your pride aside and listen to Lady Ellen," Hamilton said.

Chambers stepped forward. "Please vacate the room, sir."

I went to pick up my notebook from the wrought iron table.

"Leave it," Stone barked at me.

"Really!" I said. The inspector's manners left a lot to be desired. Still, I left the book on the table. "I can't leave my dog here."

Lottie sniffed and wiped her eyes as she went to the bedroom to fetch Prince. Hamilton took him from her and put a reassuring hand on her shoulder.

I put my arm around her after Hamilton took Prince to the door and we walked along the corridor. "Don't worry, this will all be soon over," I reassured Lottie.

"Please go to the Seaview Restaurant," Chambers said, interrupting us. "And you, my lady, come with me."

Once out of the lift, he led me to Breckon's office.

"Surely I'm no longer your prime suspect?" I asked before sitting down.

"It's all a matter of facts and motive," Chambers said." You had the biggest motive and it's the sure way to ascertain the killer. A strong motive for eradicating someone."

"But I've no real reason to kill him at all. He didn't owe me money, he wasn't blackmailing me, all I wished was for the man to leave me alone. I was nowhere near his bowl of soup, unlike other suspects."

"Inspector Stone will make things clear," Chambers said.

"So why have you not arrested me if he thinks I'm guilty?"

"We're waiting for the evidence. The inspector will advise me when he's ready for us."

I sighed and sat with the sergeant for what seemed like forever. It was at least one whole hour. During this time, I asked the man about his family to while away the time. In the distance, no doubt coming from the Seaview Restaurant, I heard Prince's barks and whines. He could clearly sense the stress of the situation, especially if Lottie was in tears. And on top of that, he was being kept from me.

Finally, Inspector Stone appeared at the door. He glanced at me. I knew in that exchange that he was pretty sure of my innocence.

"Go to the Seaview Restaurant," he ordered.

"You trust me not to escape then, Inspector?" I said as I stood up.

He huffed and waited for me to leave and closed the door behind him, to no doubt brief Chambers.

When I reached the Seaview Restaurant, I paused at the door. Constable Ryan stood on guard; he allowed me to pass. Inside were all of the suspects. Mae and Gilbert sat together at one table.

Norma was crying. "Do you think he still thinks it was me?" she said as Breckon comforted her.

Prince barked and bounded over to me. As I stroked him I watched Olive, her eyes darting around the room, her teeth worrying at her bottom lip.

Mrs Flint arrived. "I've been told to bring refreshments," she said, then frowned as she looked around the room. Her face lit up when she saw Gilbert Barry before her cheeks flushed red.

Stone and Chambers entered the room.

"Please be seated, Mrs Flint," Stone barked.

"Me?" she said.

"Yes, you." He stared at her then turned to the uniformed officer. "Ryan?"

Ryan closed the door and stood before it, blocking the only exit, save a jump from the window which opened out onto the cliff top. Chambers took a seat.

"Sit," Stone boomed at Flint and myself. I had no wish to be treated like royalty, but he was taking it a step too far.

We both found separate tables. I sat close to Lottie and Hamilton.

Stone placed my notebook on the nearest table to him. I shook my head, realising he was now going to take everything I had collated and solve the mystery, whilst taking the credit. I smiled to myself. That was fine by me. My sole purpose had been to clear mine and Hamilton's names.

Stone paced the room and adopted his monotone voice. "I've brought you all together so we can conclude the investigation." He walked around the room with his hands behind his back. "When we first spoke to you all, everyone denied having links to Major Albert Coltrane. However, honesty is clearly not an attribute of the guests or staff at Millar's Hotel."

Those present exchanged looks. It appeared that no one wanted to interrupt and draw attention to themselves.

"We have recently received a specific detail from the pathologist."

I looked up, taking an interest. I would not find this detail in my notebook and I felt goosebumps on my arms in anticipation.

"The stomach and passages of Major Albert Coltrane held no trace of soup."

I let the realisation sink in and shook my head. It had been blatantly obvious, and I'd missed it. I knew exactly what Stone was going to say next.

"The last substance Coltrane consumed was whisky."

Breckon's jaw dropped.

Olive put her hand to her mouth.

Gilbert shifted in his seat.

"It wasn't my soup. I told you!" Norma said with relief as she looked at Breckon. As he took a handkerchief from his suit jacket, she frowned.

"I took him a bottle of whisky," Breckon said.

He was interrupted by Inspector Stone. "You'll have a chance to speak. But not yet!"

"What are you saying?" Mrs Flint asked with a worried expression upon her face.

"Ha." Stone gave a short laugh. "The picture of

innocence, aren't you Mrs Flint." He swept his arm around the room. "You all had a motive to kill him."

I shook my head. He would say that, having read my notebook.

He pointed to me in a rather rude fashion. "You, the jilted lover who accused him of murdering your husband and took it upon yourself to start an amateur investigation to put us off the scent."

I shook my head. "You know I never killed him."

"Don't interrupt!" Stone shouted.

I sighed and allowed him to continue. He was clearly enjoying the experience. Feeling the tension of those present, torturing everyone, making them think they were his prime suspect.

"You were heard threatening him, with your lover." He stopped at Hamilton.

"Lady Ellen is a respectable and titled lady," Hamilton said. "We have never…"

"Then," Stone continued, "there is Norma Lloyd, the cook. Who made no secret that she hated the victim and had further reason to kill the man as she has been having an illicit affair with the manager of this hotel, who owed Coltrane a substantial amount of money."

Everyone turned to gawp at Norma and Breckon.

"Is this true?" Mrs Flint said. "Whatever will the Millars say when they return? You know it's against the rules."

Norma blushed. "That's no reason to kill a man. Our love life is hardly going to make The Gazette." She shook her head.

"True," Stone said." He pointed at Breckon. "You, sir, are a gambler and a bad one at that, if Coltrane beat you. If he told your employer, your job would be lost."

"Mr Breckon," Mrs Flint said. "You know James Millar detests gambling."

"Mrs Flint," Breckon said with a splutter. "Have some respect."

"A bottle of whisky was delivered by Mr Breckon to the victim's room." Stone said. "You had the opportunity to poison it. And the opportunity to administer the fatal dose before he even got near the suspected bowl of soup. You were probably unaware that the poison takes time to kill."

"John, you didn't," Norma gasped, leaning away from her lover. "And you let them arrest me?" She stood up.

Mrs Flint walked over and put her arm around Norma. "John Breckon, how could you!"

"Hang on," Norma said. "I saw Major Coltrane with the whisky –"

"Be quiet," Stone said. "And sit down." Stone gestured at the women before continuing to pace the room while they retook their seats. He continued. "The poison had to come from somewhere. It's not rat poison, arsenic or cyanide. This is a poison straight off the black market."

I looked over to Olive who already had tears streaming down her face.

"It is unidentifiable and likely to be an experimental drug designed for war. Someone with links to the underground would have acquired it. Someone like you…" He paused.

Everyone looked around the room as he pointed across it.

"Coltrane's lover, Olive Cox," Stone said.

"I'm innocent, it's not me. I didn't know it was poison." She put her hands to her face.

"Your innocence, young lady will be decided in court."

Lottie left her seat to console Olive.

"Inspector Stone, Olive is a very young woman. I heard her being threatened," I said. "She needs to be protected." My heart thudded as I considered what could happen to her. "I trust you will be locking up a certain person?" I felt I did not want to utter Simon Crow's name after what I had heard.

"But," Inspector Stone continued, ignoring me, "Olive Cox was a mere cog in this crime. The poison has been located. He opened a bag on the table, put on a pair of black gloves and lifted out a blue glass bottle.

Mrs Flint gasped.

"Exactly, Mrs Flint – you have been exposed."

"That's not poison, it's perfume," she said, then looked sheepishly at Gilbert Barry, who looked back with a confused expression on his face.

"Of course it is," Stone said in a sarcastic tone. "And where did you come by this perfume, Mrs Flint?"

She looked again to Gilbert and then back to the inspector. "I bought it at the market."

I sat back, waiting for Inspector Stone's reaction. Mrs Flint was clearly lying, I knew it and the inspector knew it. She'd taken it from Gilbert's room as a collectable.

"You would do anything for Gilbert Barry," Mr Stone said. "A man you idolise like a crazy woman."

"It was in the bin," she protested.

"We will come to that," he said. "So, now I would like to turn to Mae and Gilbert. Esteemed guests and national heroes who have graced us with their presence." Sarcasm dripped from his voice.

"Inspector, if you carry on like this, your theatrics will put us out of business," Gilbert said with a laugh, acting extremely cool for a soon-to-be-accused man. "Now come on man, tell us who committed the murder so we can be on our way. We have a show to put on…" He looked at his wristwatch. "…in two hours. So do hurry along, chap."

The inspector's eyes widened and he thrust his arm out. "You, sir, will be taken from here and kept in close confinement…"

"What do you mean?" Gilbert asked as the smile slipped from his face.

"You, Gilbert Barry, are a cold blooded murderer."

Gilbert stood up. "What?"

Mae blinked. "Father? Tell me this isn't true?"

"Father?" Mrs Flint said aghast.

We all looked on as Stone smirked at me, glancing down at the entry I had made in my notebook, which stated that I suspected Mae was Gilbert's daughter and the little girl, Emma, back in Yorkshire, was actually his granddaughter.

"Yes indeed," Stone said with a smug look, as if he had worked it all out for himself and not just read my words. "Gilbert Barry is the father of Mae Grey, also known as Maude Green. A young Maude became pregnant by Coltrane when she was a dancing girl."

I caught Mae's expression and she looked devastated, clearly believing I had given the inspector that information.

"After seeking out her real father, he and his wife took in her child and passed her off as their own daughter."

"How dare you talk of my daughter as if she is from the gutter."

"Father had no idea about me," Mae sobbed. "My mother told me the name of my father on her death bed. She did not know where to find him, he was a young travelling actor when she knew him. And then she saw him on stage and by that time he was married. She was a good woman who did not want to ruin his life."

"A good woman?" The inspector laughed, then pointed to Gilbert. "*He* killed Coltrane, who was going to reveal those details to the press."

"Coltrane never knew!" Mae said, then looked at Gilbert who hung his head. "Father, no!"

Gilbert glanced back to her. "I told the blasted man. He accused me of having an affair with you. I argued with him at Jake's Jazz Bar a week or so ago, when I'd had too much whisky, and blurted it out that you were not my lover, you were my daughter." He ran a finger over his moustache. "From that moment, he began blackmailing me." He looked up at the inspector. "But I tell you man, I never killed him and have not seen that bottle of poison before."

"I'm afraid I do not believe that, Mr Barry. And not only that, you also had an accomplice. Your maniac admirer, Mrs Ina Flint." He pointed at her.

"That's not true!" Mrs Flint began to cry and this time Norma comforted her.

"Is this really necessary, Inspector?" I said and stood up. "You have managed to drag everyone present through the dirt. Detailing personal secrets for your own satisfaction. I'm sure no one is perfect in this life and we all have secrets. I'm sure you have some yourself." I raised my eyebrows as if I knew something about him. Of course, I didn't, but he faltered for a moment before I turned away and continued. "Do you gain pleasure from lording it over those you see as better off than yourself?" I paused, realising maybe I had gone a step too far.

"I'll have you arrested, woman." Stone spat his words at me.

"What for?" I asked. "Speaking the truth?"

Hamilton jumped up. "Inspector, take a breath." Then he caught my eye, as if the instruction should also apply to me.

Stone stared at me, flaring his nostrils like a bull about to attack, as I turned back and faced him.

I shook my head. "Not only have you stolen my notebook and spilled the details of these people's private lives in a most salacious way, you've arrived at the totally wrong conclusion." I took a breath. "Sergeant Chambers spoke to me earlier." I gestured at him. "He said that it's all a matter facts and motive. And he was right."

Chambers nodded at me. "Thank you, my lady." Clearly Chambers was also tiring of Inspector Stone.

"Come on then, your...ladyship. What happened?" Stone demanded.

"One person acquired a bottle of poison. The same person acquired a bottle of whisky and that person also planned a murder."

"Who?" Mae asked, looking around the room at everyone individually and then back at me.

"Major Albert Coltrane," I said.

"He killed himself?" Mae asked with a gasp.

Inspector Stone gave a slow clap. "Well done, Lady Ellen. Convince us all it was suicide, thinking you'll get away with it." He lifted my notebook. "Preparing this as smoke and mirrors. Hoping it will all go away and then you can return to your cosy life in your mansion. You've led us up the garden path with this fiction, pointing us in the wrong direction and planting evidence. Chambers... Arrest this woman for murder."

I spoke in a measured tone. "Just listen to me." I stared at Chambers, who took a step backwards.

"If you don't mind, Inspector," Chambers said. "I'd like to hear her ladyship out before making an arrest."

I glanced around the room. All eyes were upon me.

"Very well," Stone said as he turned away and walked to the window with his arms crossed, staring out to sea.

"Major Albert Coltrane was a despicable man," I said. "Who thought nothing of killing to get to what he wanted." I paused, remembering Leonard, but I did not want to make this personal. "In this case, he wanted Mae Grey – a successful woman who has worked hard to reinvent herself and to be where she is today. He wanted her, but most importantly, he wanted her money and an easy lifestyle."

Mae shook her head. "Never, would I have ever…"

"One thing that Coltrane did not lack was self-confidence. He viewed himself as a catch and thought that it was only Mr Barry stopping him from getting to Mae. He tried to befriend him by playing him at cards but only succeeded in getting himself into debt. He tried blackmailing him but that also did not work."

"I told him to get lost," Gilbert said. "I wasn't going to pay him a penny, he owed me. He backed off then and said he would pay me back."

I nodded. "Coltrane had motive. He contacted the black market and acquired a bottle of deadly poison, which he had delivered here to the hotel. Olive had no knowledge of the contents of the package. Coltrane simply used her as a mule, not wanting any physical contact with the unsavoury Simon Crow.

Norma gasped as the sound of his name.

"On that fateful night, Coltrane ordered a nice

bottle of malt from the hotel, asking Mr Breckon to add it to his bill and deliver it to his room. Once in his possession, Coltrane took the bottle of whisky and the poison, disguised as a bottle of perfume which he could easily conceal on his person, to Gilbert's room with the intention of poisoning him to death."

Mae clutched her father's arm.

I turned to Gilbert. "When I saw you at your birthday party, we had a conversation about Coltrane."

He frowned. "So we did."

"And you told me that Coltrane was such a miser that when he poured whisky, he gave himself a larger glass and his guest the smaller one. But you did not let him get away with that."

"That's true. Yes, I said to him, I only drink whisky on ice and as he turned for the bucket of ice in my room, I picked up the glass with the larger serving for him to plop the ice into."

The room fell silent as we all digested that information.

Gilbert spoke in a small voice. "'Down in one,' Coltrane had said. 'The only way to drink it.' I watched him do just that and then followed suit as he kept his eyes on me."

"You saved yourself from a poisoned glass of whisky," I said.

"How awful," Mae said.

"He really did want me dead!" Gilbert sat back in his chair.

"Indeed," I said.

"Thank goodness, I say, for the Branden Bay ice house." Gilbert gave a nervous laugh, trying to lighten the mood, but he was visibly shocked.

Mae put her arms around her father. "We could have lost you."

"And then the evidence went missing, as Mrs Flint here…" I motioned to her.

Mrs Flint flushed a deep red. "I'm so sorry if I hindered the investigation when I took the empty glasses as a keepsake and the…" She lowered her voice, "…poison. I honestly thought it was perfume when I found it in Gilbert's bin. I must say it was rather odd smelling. I wore it the other day."

"Was that the day you were incredibly ill, by any chance?" I asked her.

Mrs Flint rubbed her neck. "Oh my goodness gracious me, I could have died!"

"Major Albert Coltrane got what he deserved," Chambers said to Stone. "I'll take it from here, Inspector, if you want to get back to your honeymoon?"

Inspector Stone turned around and peered at me as if he wanted to throw an insult, but appeared to have nothing at hand as he left the room without a further word.

As soon as he was gone, Hamilton clapped and the others joined in. "Well done, Lady Ellen."

Prince barked and jumped up at me.

"Before we disperse," I said, "I'd just like to ask everyone to please keep Mae and Gilbert's secrets quiet."

"We're planning to come clean," Mae said. "About Gilbert being my father. I'm fed up with the comments about us being lovers. Everything else will hopefully remain private."

"I'm rather thinking of writing this whole episode into a play," Gilbert said.

"Dad, no!" Mae said then laughed as everyone joined in.

"I don't know about anyone else," Hamilton said. "But I could really do with a drink."

"Whisky anyone?" Gilbert said.

"No!" came the collective response.

CHAPTER 22

*W*ith three days of rest and late mornings, I felt suitably refreshed and pleased that I could finally begin my stress-free break at Millar's Hotel. I lay on my bed with the curtains open, looking up at the blue sky. Following the resolution of the case, I had managed to convince Sergeant Chambers to relocate Olive Cox. He agreed that she would be in grave danger if Simon Crow got hold of her. That very night when he had signed off duty, Chambers had driven Olive and her father to Ashcombe Hall, with a letter from myself to Mrs Dawkins asking her to find discreet employment for them within my grounds. I knew they would have to move on again if Crow got wind of it, but until word got out about their whereabouts, they would be safe. I had not even divulged this information to Lottie or Hamilton. Chambers said that other than us two, no one would find out.

There was a knock at the door of my bedroom.

"It's me," Lottie called out.

"Come in." I sat up in the bed.

She opened the door. "Lady Ellen, would you still like breakfast in your room?" Lottie asked as Prince woofed in the background, sounding as if he had enjoyed his morning walk along the beach.

"Let's take breakfast downstairs and we can discuss sightseeing."

Prince squeezed past Lottie and bounded over to me and jumped on the bed. I laughed as I stroked his coat, finding traces of sand in it, a tell-tale sign that he had probably rolled around on the beach. The maid would have to sweep the room.

"Shall I ask Captain Hamilton to join us?" she asked with a smile.

"Please do." I had not seen an awful lot of Hamilton since we had discovered what had happened to Major Coltrane. "I understand he has three weeks before his next job, so he will be at a loose end."

"It's not just that, my lady. I'm sure he wants to spend a lot more time with you before he has to go."

I turned away and glanced at my reflection in the mirror, noticing the blush cover my face. I also noted that Lottie was shifting her feet, looking extremely sheepish.

I turned around. "What is it, Lottie?" I asked.

"Can I invite Sebastian sightseeing? He's planning on coming here again at the weekend. His aunt, uncle and cousin are going on a trip without him, so he's free for a few days."

I wasn't quite sure that encouraging this romance was a good thing, even though Lottie was no longer engaged to Joseph Flint. Mrs Flint did not have a problem with the girl now and I wondered whether she had told Lottie's aunt that she was no longer keeping a beady eye on Lottie. Flint was planning a short holiday to Exeter to watch Joseph on stage, with all expenses paid by Gilbert Barry who was feeling extremely generous after his dice with death.

"Very well," I said. "But at some point, maybe I need to have a word with young Sebastian."

"Great." Lottie beamed. "I will write and let him know."

Prince barked.

Lottie stroked him. "You like Sebastian too, don't you boy?"

"And Lottie," I said.

"Yes my lady?" she looked up at me.

I smiled at her. "Please, from now on, there's no need to call me my lady or Lady Ellen. Please simply call me Ellen."

She rushed over and wrapped her arms around me in a tight hug, which was so sweet it brought tears to my eyes. "Thank you, my lady." She laughed as she released me. "I mean, Ellen."

LATER, as Lottie, myself and Prince reached the ground floor, there was a commotion as a man with a tanned face stood in the reception, seemingly checking in along with a glamorous woman and a young man. "What's with this death I've been told about by the chauffeur?" he demanded, shouting at Breckon, who had for some days appeared stress free.

"Everything is under control," Breckon said.

Lottie stood half behind me, as if hiding, and Price remained unusually quiet as well. Probably taking in the sights and smells of these new people and their huge collection of luggage.

I thought I'd brought a lot of luggage, I thought. *This is excessive.*

The blonde middle-aged woman huffed as she passed us. "I'm going to my suite and have no intention of appearing for a week. We need to recuperate. Come along, James."

The man with the tanned face followed her and sighed as he passed. "Insufferable woman," he said then called out: "Breckon, show Thomas to his room."

The young man looked around the reception in awe. He appeared older than Sebastian and looked to be in his early twenties. "This is great."

"This way, Mr Jenkins," Breckon said. "Your uncle has said he wishes all three of you to keep to your rooms until you are rested. I'll arrange room service."

Breckon led the young man towards the lift.

The porter dragged one of the huge trunks they had brought with them, shaking his head.

"The Millars are back," Lottie said.

"Ah," I said. "That explains the amount of luggage."

"Norma told me they were bringing their nephew back. James Millar's nephew, Thomas. His sister's boy."

"I'm thirsty," Thomas Jenkins said as he reached the lift and turned away. Breckon followed the young man as he headed for the hotel bar.

"Norma said she senses a storm," Lottie said.

"I do hope not," I said as I laughed and led Lottie to the Seaview Restaurant for a hearty breakfast. I wanted to plan what I hoped would be some fun weeks ahead.

Hamilton stood up as we approached the table he had reserved for us and I sat down, taking in the view. I smiled at him.

Prince nuzzled my hand and I stroked his head. "Yes boy, we're going to have a super time now that we can finally relax."

IF YOU ENJOYED the first book in the Lady Ellen Investigates series, join Ellen, Hamilton, Lottie, Sebastian and Prince for their next investigation to find *A Killer at the Castle*

Can Ellen finally savour a relaxing break at Millar's Hotel? Not quite. Her plans take an unexpected turn when a sightseeing tour of Branden Bay Castle turns deadly.

The picturesque castle stands proudly above the town and beach. Ellen finds herself thrust into the heart of a chilling mystery when a poor soul plummets from one of the castle's turrets. On a blustery day, it seems like a dreadful accident, but the police suspect foul play.

As the victim's will is unveiled, a shock revelation exposes drama, indiscretions, and disputes. Motives lay bare and Ellen is called upon to untangle the truth. Alongside Lottie, Hamilton, Sebastian and Prince, Ellen must unravel the truth.

Order *A Killer at the Castle*

IF YOU WOULD LIKE to read the prequel and find out how Ellen met Hamilton and rescued Prince from a fate many runts faced visit https://subscribepage.io/ Kellysnews

ACKNOWLEDGMENTS

I'd like to thank my creative writing tutor Rosemary Dun, both inside the OU and out! You encouraged me to pursue novel writing and gave me so much information and guidance, I'm still reading the handouts! You are amazing. Thanks also goes to my brilliant mentors Alison Knight and Jenny Kane of Imagine Creative Writing and their Novel in a Year course, which gave me lots of help and kept me on track.

Thanks to the inspirational friends I met through the Romantic Novelists' Association, and the Bristol writing community (I'm too scared to list everyone in case I miss someone off!) And to my Beta readers, Tara Starling, Cinnomen Matthews McGuigan, Michelle Armitage, Tara Starling, Shell Rice Mortimer and Leanne Goodall. Thanks also to Helen Blenkinsop who is a guru on the 'hook' and amazon ads. And thanks to my best writing friends – Callie Hill, Claire O'Conner and Jenny Treasure, for also being beta readers and for sharing the journey with me. And to my Women's Fic mastermind and my accountability partner Soraya. My Editor Becky Halls. And not forgetting my two author mates, Laura and Andy who make life fun!

Thank you to my advance reader team who are

really supportive and there for me, even from the first book.

Thank you to those on my mailing list who interact with me.

Thanks to my family for supporting me, especially Gary for putting up with me tapping away at the keyboard 24/7.